AVA CUVAY

SILVER CYBORG SERIES BOOK ONE

TIN MAN

Dedication

*To my husband, my hero, my love. The man who can fix anything.
To my children and their awesome sense of humor. Three words:
walk this way.
To my author friends and all their support and cheerleading!*

Acknowledgements

*Thank you to my writing pal Kitt Rose. For helping me to
brainstorm this book. For your creativity and badass technology
skills. For your support and patience. And, always, for your
quirky humor!*

*Thank you to the rest of my Dream Team: Cindy Tanner and
Melanie Jayne. Your dedication, hard work, humor, wisdom, and
support are priceless!*

*Thank you to my Critique Partners, Liza Jonathan and Kitt Rose,
for your insight and suggestions for Tin Man. Thank you to my
Beta Reader Kelly Snyder with Twinsie Talk for your honesty and
support. Thank you to my Editor Nan Reinhardt for your
teaching and encouragement. Thank you to my cover artist
Fiona Jayde for this amazing cover! And Thank you to my
Whorecrux Resisters for all the hilarious inappropriateness!*

You ladies are THE BEST!!

Chapter One

A slow start to the night promises a crazy ending… said no one ever. But, based on his years as a bouncer at the historic Vogue Bar and Music Venue, Adam Lehmann knew the saying was truth. This Saturday night shift was downright dull so far, and the tingle in his lower back—the part which didn't have cybernetic sensors running through it—assured him tonight was doomed.

He didn't yet know what or why, but something would swerve into shit creek territory, and the cops would be called.

Cops who had once been his friends and coworkers. Guys who'd had his back. Up until part of that back, his heart, his left arm, and an eye had been replaced with cybernetics. On the outside, Adam didn't look any different than he had. But simply knowing he wasn't entirely organic beneath the epidermis layer was enough to make him an object of fear and loathing.

The awkward shift from pal to *persona non grata* hadn't been listed as a possible side effect when he'd allowed doctors to replace his shot-to-hell body parts with experimental cyborg systems. If it had, he might have let himself die on the operating table. Scratch that, he would have assumed his friendships were tight enough to withstand a few synthetic enhancements.

The joke was on him. And it wasn't funny.

"You seem on edge, Lemon." The automaton bartender handed him a bottle of water. Adam forced a neutral expression at the slight mispronunciation, which turned his last name into a proclamation of his derelict physical state. Adam's glitching cyborg parts and mid-forties human body did not mesh well. A mid-life crises of epic proportions with no hope of coming out on the other side any way but dead. Not that he would admit that to anyone.

"I *seem?* A bit of a subjective statement, don't you think Arthur?"

Arthur's robotic Swiss army knife body rotated beneath its head, its multiple attachments a symphony of cleaning, stacking, filling, pouring, serving. Only its face held any humanoid features, and those looked like the poor schmuck who passed out first at a fraternity party. Someone had taken a black marker to the mechanized bartender, decorating it with a scraggly goatee, handlebar mustache, scars, anime eyelashes, a black eye, and the word *dildo* in bold caps across his forehead. Instead of paying to have the synthetic covering cleaned or replaced, The Vogue's owner had shrugged at the vandalism and invested in costume hats to add to Arthur's look. Tonight, it sported a red bandana skull cap and pirate eye-patch. Adam refused to laugh at the ridiculousness of it.

To be honest, he didn't laugh, period. Looming demise did that to a person.

"Incorporating common human phrases and word usage is part of my programming." Arthur's artificially generated voice was an unemotional monotone. "Your pupils are dilated 38 percent, your heartrate increased 25 percent, and your shoulders have lowered point-five inches. All symptoms of tension. As you have often lamented your lack of personal activities, I conclude it is work related."

"Lamented? Is that another common word usage you've incorporated?" Adam twisted the bottle open with a flick of his wrist. "Don't recall ever *lamenting* anything, although I have mentioned my short list of hobbies."

Arthur paused in its multi-tasking for a moment. "Lamented seemed the appropriate word for your condition."

Lamented. Seemed. "Better take care, talking like that." Adam murmured the warning over the top of the bottle. "You might be mistaken for a human."

Adam knew better than anyone, humans did not take kindly to being impersonated. Their need to play god and create something in their own image warred with their fear of creating something which might render them unnecessary. This explained why automechs enjoyed a spotty sort of popularity, while alpha-phase cyborg transitions such as himself were pariahs.

He choked down the ugly cocktail of envy and bitterness burning in his chest. The fact Arthur's creators were fearful hypocrites wasn't its fault. The automech merely fulfilled its programming. Adam shrugged off his harsh opinion—although they no longer claimed him, he was also a member of that human race—and changed the subject. "I got a bad feeling about this, Arthur. The night's gonna jump the rails at some point."

"That is illogical, as *night* is a term for a period of planetary rotation in relation to the sun, not an obsolete transport vehicle requiring directionally guided tracks. And please, call me Artie."

Arthur made the request nightly, oblivious to the fact the nickname was a slur against all Artificial Intelligent automechs. Whoever had named it Arthur to begin with had played a joke Adam found distasteful on behalf of the robot. Or maybe because the insult hit a little too close to home. "*Jump the rails* is a common human phrase, Arthur."

"Not anymore. That specific idiom fell out of usage nearly three decades ago."

Feeling every day of his forty-four years, Adam took a long swig of the crisp water and scanned the sparse crowd. The current patrons consisted of a group of students from nearby Butler University ribbing each other over a game of *dejarik*, some locals laughing at the holo-darts, and a middle-aged woman fidgeting at one of the corner tables. A subdued, unremarkable scene, like a calm lake. A deep well of water which would swell, building pressure until bursting like a broken dam once the night's band was into their third set, bringing death, destruction, and panic with it.

Yep, crazy would happen tonight, right in the middle of Indianapolis's eclectic Old Broad Ripple Village bar scene.

Adam ground his molars at the possibility of having to interact with his former fellow officers tonight. The wary looks, like he would suddenly go all rogue-robot-murdering-spree on them, thank you Hollywood for that fucking paranoia. In truth, he was more likely to seize up and die on them like granddad's rusty truck, although he kept the tidbit to himself. Still, his gut churned in foreboding that tonight would get out of hand.

"I see you are scoping out the possible threats." Arthur piped up. Apparently, AI mechs yearned for conversation to distract them from their menial jobs. "My vote is an alcohol-inspired brawl between the two groups."

Possible. Too much alcohol made people stupid and unpredictable. But Adam's gut told him that wouldn't be the case. He shook his head, calling upon his years of police-force training to examine the subtle behaviors of the guys at the *dejarik* board. Nothing aggressive or defensive from any of them. His programming ran their stances and motions against his database of universal body language psychology. He switched his cyborg corneal lens between infrared, ultraviolet, and magnification. He noticed the untouched condensation on the near-full beer bottles. His gut was right.

"Unlikely we'll get a bar fight from those guys. They're probably just killing time until their girlfriends arrive. Then they'll go someplace trendier."

"What about the crowd at the holo-darts? Money is being exchanged. No doubt they are gambling and someone is going to get accused of cheating."

"You gunning for my job, Arthur?" Adam snorted. He wasn't much for idle conversation. "This isn't the Old West. There won't be a showdown in the streets. How about you stick to pouring drinks and let me watch the drunks?"

"Very well. But if I am right, you owe me a new hat."

Adam's lips twitched at that.

Normally, his scowl and powerful build were enough to keep trouble at bay. He got to toss a rowdy drunk or handsy college boy on occasion. Pour a giggling bachelorette party into a cab. Once in a great while, he redirected the determined attention of a woman too deep in her cups to realize she was beer-goggling an alpha-phase cyborg. Just normal bouncing business which he could handle with one robotically-enhanced arm tied behind his back.

But tonight? Tonight would be one of those jacked-all-to-hell nights. His Spidey-senses said so.

The lone woman at the corner table was what he would consider *a person of interest*. And not just because she was attractive. Her gaze skittered around the room, never landing on anything for more than a moment. She turned her glass of white wine in her hands without drinking. Her shoulders hunched as if trying to make herself as small as possible, to avoid notice. A difficult task, since she was not the bar's typical clientele. Older. Classier. Pricier clothes. Attractive enough to stand out in a packed house.

He pushed off the bar rail and headed toward her. He

wouldn't admit to Arthur, but Adam was pretty certain she'd be at the eye of the evening's shit storm. At least, that's what the tingle in his spine and hitch in his breathing told him each time he glanced her way.

Or maybe those physical reactions were desire. He hadn't experienced that particular sensation in so long, it was easily confused with something else. Yet every time he saw the rich auburn of her shoulder-length hair, his fingers itched to run through its thick waves. Even the synthetic circuits in his left hand flinched. Each time his gaze paused at her full lips, an electric zap of need shot to his groin. Like applying a defibrillator to a dead man, his cock jerked to life.

Adam gritted his teeth and willed the undead zombie in his pants back into the grave. His body rarely obeyed him these days, malfunctioning at the most inopportune times. He nearly stumbled when his penis settled down to sleep again. Great, the one body part he wouldn't mind being livelier was happy to keep napping.

The woman eyed him warily as he crossed the bar and slid onto the chair across from her. Brown eyes like English toffee ringed with chocolate framed by long dark lashes continued to glance around the room, but settled on him more often than not. Adam forced his breathing to keep steady as his mechanical heart kicked a rapid beat. Was it malfunctioning? If he keeled over dead right here, everyone would discover he was a cyborg, and he'd worked so hard to hide the fact. But that wouldn't matter if he was dead, right?

"Can I help you?" Her sultry voice rolled over his senses like velvet. His zombie cock lurched. His brain frizzed and froze, no answer to her question coming forth.

Adam leaned forward, resting his forearms on the table, stalling and hoping his cerebral malfunction was brief. She leaned back against the seat, away from him and maybe making room for a quick getaway. Distrusting and nervous. He tried for a good-cop smile. "Blind date?"

"Blind date?" Her brows furrowed and the effect was adorable. She was a beautiful woman. Heart-shaped face, high cheekbones, arched eyebrows. She'd applied her makeup with a light and expert hand. Faint laugh lines at the corner of her eyes and one off-center worry crease between her brows. Older than the bar's typical patron, especially given the heavy metal band slated for tonight. Possibly in her late thirties, maybe early forties.

He leaned back to appear relaxed and unconcerned. "Yeah, are you waiting for a blind date? Related to one of the band members? Lost? Are you sure you're supposed to be *here*?"

Anger flickered in her eyes. "Is there a law against me being here?"

"Not at all. We just don't often get customers like you."

One eyebrow rose and her lips formed a thin line. "Like me."

Shit, he'd pissed her off. He might be a good bouncer, but standing and glaring for a living was affecting his people skills. Or maybe the light floral scent of her perfume was shorting out his micro-processor. He shook his head. "No offense, but classy and beautiful women usually avoid this bar. Especially on night's when Satan's Rage is playing."

Her eyebrow lowered, but her cautious expression remained. "Are you saying I can't be a deathcore metalhead and wear Javier Anolo pumps at the same time?"

Some trendy shoe designer he'd seen advertised somewhere. Yep, she was undeniably out of his class. "I'm saying the head thrashing will mess up your hairdo."

She patted her hair self-consciously at the mention of it. "I am meeting someone. Not a date, *per se*. Just someone I've met online. And we agreed it would be nice to meet in person."

She met his gaze directly, after having avoided eye contact through her confession. He didn't require twenty years on the beat or his cybernetic systems to know she wasn't giving him the truth. At least not all of it. Adam's heart cheered at the knowledge she wasn't waiting for a date to arrive, which was a weird reaction to have. He didn't know this woman, and shouldn't care about her immediate plans, much less be happy they weren't on the romantic end of the spectrum.

He ran a hand through his hair, and propped his elbow on the chair back. "So, what's your friend's name? What does your friend look like? When she—he?—shows up at the door, I'll escort 'em over and save you all that awkward watching and wondering and waiting for the other person."

Her expensive suit jacket hid her figure, but he guessed she was tall and trim. She adjusted it and he caught a glimpse of a cream satin shirt beneath it. She looked like she'd come straight from her office job, even though tonight was Saturday. Likely one of those career-minded execs who worked eighty-hour weeks. Intelligent, professional, and capable.

If he had a "type," she would be it. Which also meant she was out of his ballpark. As a bouncer, he didn't belong in the dating major leagues. As a cyborg, he didn't get to play the game. Hiding his cybernetic status meant building a relationship on a shaky foundation. Add in the fact his mechanical heart hindered his ability to feel the tender emotions a girlfriend would expect. The most he could hope for was a good fuck, but his glitching made that little bit of contact risky. Yet he couldn't stop the temptation to scan her heat signature in hopes she—

Shit. His cyborg eye glitched and went dark. He could bang it against the wall to jar it back online, but would have to wait until he had a private moment. Wouldn't do for her, or anyone else, to see him bash his head like some wacko.

Further proof of how this night would go.

She clicked her short, unpainted fingernails—no rings on any fingers—against the wineglass, then put her hands in her lap while her gaze swept the room again. She was obviously nervous as hell, but that didn't narrow down to *why*. If she was a naturally shy person—he doubted she was—meeting a practical stranger in an unfamiliar bar would be nerve-wracking.

"I imagine you'll be too busy with your regular duties tonight to provide such personal service." Her chin lifted a notch and she cleared her throat. "But your offer is very considerate and I appreciate the thought, Mister… Uh… Mister—?"

"Just call me Adam. Adam Lehmann. At your service." He forced his eyes to meet hers, and not look where she nibbled her plump bottom lip.

"Adam. Thank you—"

"And you are?"

"Oh. Um, I'm Evelyn… Eve… So, thank you for the offer, but I don't know what my acquaintance looks like. Or his real name. I only know his online handle."

She might not be here for a date *per se*, but there was a man involved, and Adam's heart grumbled. The damn thing was a cybernetic replacement and shouldn't be cheering or grumbling or doing anything but beating. He was definitely malfunctioning. Unless he could determine if her plans might adversely impact the general business of the bar and its patrons, he shouldn't be concerned with their details. His job was to keep the peace so the bar patrons could enjoy their evening, not ferret out personal drama. Reeling his emotions back in, he leaned on his interrogation skills. "You don't know what he looks like or his real name. But yet you decided it was a good idea to meet face-to-face?"

One eyebrow rose again, likely in response to the accusatory tone of his voice. She responded with ice. "All relationships begin with two strangers meeting, Mr. Lehmann."

He turned his hands palms-up in deference. "Forgive an old bouncer for being jaded. I see more of the shady side of human interactions than I care to admit."

Why the fuck had he referred to himself as *old?*

The eyebrow lowered again and she mushed her lips

together. Twisting the wine stem between her fingers, she glanced toward the stage, but her focus seemed inward. "I'm sorry for being snippy. The truth is I'm nervous. The safety net of anonymity an online relationship brings isn't there when you meet someone in person. And I… I question whether I've made the right decision."

Adam couldn't fault her logic, nor did he want to berate her uncertainty. Unbidden, his left hand reached across the table toward her. He managed to stop it and lay his palm flat before he touched her. "What's your friend's online handle?"

"MadDog2020." She grimaced as if she realized the absurdity of her situation.

MadDog2020? Why would anyone name themselves after a low-end liquor that hadn't been made in over a century? What was the meaning behind it? Why not pick Mead1300? Or BoonesFarm2110? The handle made no sense, and by the way her lips thinned into a mulish line, she'd said more than she felt comfortable sharing. Best to wait her out a bit.

He nodded and rose from the table. "Well, Eve, it's a pleasure to meet you. And as security for this establishment, I commend you for choosing the safety of a public location to meet someone you barely know. If, at any point, you feel uncomfortable or unsafe, please know I'm here all night. It wouldn't be the first time I've discouraged an overly attentive date or escorted a woman to her car to ensure her safety. Otherwise, I hope you enjoy your evening."

She slid her top lip against her bottom lip, a motion she did a lot and which seemed to be her physical outlet for her nervousness. Adam tucked that insightful tidbit away. After a moment, she jerked her head in a stilted nod. He wandered back to his post at the front door and considered the possible ways she might ask for his assistance, cursing his libido for tossing in several carnal options. He needed to spend the evening keeping peace at the bar, not in his pants.

Chapter Two

Know I'm here all night. Those words hung heavy in the air around Eve, like a sultry dream, having been uttered in a low, morning-after rumble with a hint of southern drawl. Fortunately, Adam hadn't used that drawl and those lips to call her *Darlin'* or she might have spilled her secrets. She'd been a sucker for southern charm since she could remember, and decades living in Chicago hadn't dimmed that preference one bit. Or offered any acceptable replacements, including her ex-husband.

She sighed and stared into her glass of warming white wine, cursing the luck which brought her to this bar to meet with MadDog and give him the micro-drive taped behind her ear. The drive held a file she'd stumbled upon while searching her employer's executive network for revised sales projections. A file she couldn't unsee. She didn't have to be a software genius like the CEO to realize this file contained damning proof her employer, Preditech, was engaged in a deadly kind of corporate corruption.

How could she be expected to walk away and pretend she didn't know the truth? So, she'd downloaded it and ridden the three hours from Chicago to Indianapolis in her self-driving car to get it into the hands of someone who could do something meaningful with its contents.

By blowing the whistle on Preditech, she was dooming hundreds of people to unemployment, jail, or financial ruin from the resulting fallout. And she'd be blacklisted, hiding for the rest of her life like some mob informant from the twentieth century.

So, no big deal, right? Stuff like that happens every day. Nothing to be worried about or stressed over. Go ahead, add in an eclectic bar-slash-music venue with a bouncer who walked straight out of her every bad-boy dream, and have him offer to look out for her like he was her personal body guard. Sure, her nerves could take it.

Who was she kidding? She was ready to crawl out of her skin.

"Please, god, let this be worth it." She muttered to the wine glass. The tape behind her ear pulled at strands of hair, reminding her why she was here. Yes, the information she'd give to MadDog would inconvenience a lot of people. But keeping the information a secret was getting people killed. Specifically, the officers and firefighters who'd volunteered their bodies for the first phase in experimental cybernetic implants. What Preditech had done was a crime, promising first-responders cybernetic parts to replace those injured in the line of duty, when the real intent had been to make them lab rats by infiltrating and undermining the functions of their own bodies.

Her coworkers might be inconvenienced by the consequences of her information, but these everyday heroes were dying.

Eve mashed her lips together, smearing her gloss sheen lipstick. A nervous habit from high school which she'd never been able to break. Fortunately, she wasn't a poker player. Hopefully Adam hadn't noticed her tell.

"If he noticed, maybe he just thinks I'm nervous about

meeting MadDog." Eve muttered into her glass, embarrassed for making conversation with her sauvignon blanc, although it was her only friend at the moment.

She gulped her wine to drown her self-pity and bolster her determination. The zesty beverage hit the back of her throat, making her cough and bringing tears to her eyes. She dabbed at the corners, taking care not to smear her mascara. She might be a nervous mess on the inside, but a brave front could get her through a chunk of problems. She'd used bravado to stare down company execs with bad ideas, an ex-husband in divorce proceedings, and the seventh-grade mean girl. She wouldn't wimp out simply because her plan to take down Preditech wasn't as cut and dried as her profit-and-loss reports.

A furtive glance around the room proved the clientele had changed. The bar was filling with a mob of young adults dressed in black and spikes, smears of dark makeup, and the holographic thought bubbles which were so trendy with today's youth. The colorful projections made the crowd resemble a Sunday paper comic, but what did she know... she was Generation Epsilon. Old enough to be their mom and therefore decidedly uncool.

When the first jarring, eardrum-stabbing chords of music crashed through the room, the mob became a thrashing, head-banging entity. Eve cringed at the discordant cacophony. Yeah, she was not the expected clientele for tonight.

She sighed and stared into the depths of her wine for clarity. Her angsty youth was too far in the rearview mirror to remember, and the past decade with Preditech had aged her more than her mere forty-two years. Once she handed her micro-drive over to MadDog, she should get lost in some small town somewhere in Middle America, get a no-pressure job, and buy a starter pack of cats. Or a dog. Some simple creature that would be thrilled to receive her attention and love and not stack undeliverable expectations and demands at her feet.

She leaned back in her chair on a bone-weary exhale and

rubbed her lips across each other again. Scanning the growing crowd, she hoped whoever this MadDog was, she'd know him when she saw him. Which she didn't. Her gaze gravitated toward Adam, like it had all evening. He was simply too enticing to ignore, standing against a far wall with his black shirt clinging to his muscled arms and his no-bullshit scowl keeping the crowd focused on the band. When he'd cornered her at the table, she'd waffled between wanting to run from him and wanting to jump him. He was a fascinating mix of authoritative and friendly, calling to her innermost yearning for an equal who was also a pillar of support. Someone who would fight with her, for her. Someone who would hold her and promise her everything would be alright when she knew full well everything was fucked. Someone who would fuck her like she was the embodiment of all their desires.

Wow, I'm horny.

As much as she tried to be inconspicuous, she couldn't stop looking at him and thrusting her own fantasies on him. Fantasies she needed to wrangle because now was not the time to indulge in them. She had to be strong and determined. And alone. Her mission was too important to get sidetracked by a hot man.

The hot man in question caught her gaze and winked. Eve gasped and looked away, her face aflame from having been caught staring. She dropped her hands to her lap and wrung her fingers, her heart racing against the sudden drop in oxygen around her. When would MadDog get here so she could get this exchange over with? If he didn't show up soon, her nerves would snap. She hadn't been this on edge since a year ago when she'd stood toe-to-toe with her ex and demanded her half of the business she'd devoutly helped him build at the expense of her own career and personal life. Instead, she'd gotten barely enough money to slink off to an empty apartment in the Chicago Hyde Park area, and had spent the following month cloistered there, hunting for a new job, drowning in pints of Häagen-Dazs self-pity, and raising a spoon to the crappy success of her court room bravado.

Where would she go to curl up and recuperate after tonight?

An automech server placed a glass of white wine on the table, jerking her from her gloomy thoughts. She hadn't ordered another glass. She still had half a glass of untouched wine. The music volume prohibited verbal communication, but all automaton servers had lip-reading recognition software programs. Still, Eve raised her voice when she spoke. "What's this?"

The screen beneath the server's robotic head scrolled her the answer. *white wine. sauvignon blanc. oliver winery.*

"I didn't order another glass of wine." She couldn't keep from yelling to be heard above the music. A human server might have mistakenly delivered another's drink order to her table, but not an automech server. Someone must have sent it, but who?

courtesy. gentleman. adam.

Heat shot to her cheeks, and to points farther south. She glanced his way, catching his gaze. He nodded at her. Dear god, he'd bought her a glass of wine. That was, like, something a man did when he was interested right? Too many years had passed since she'd been hit on. She barely remembered the rules of engagement. "Um. Please extend my gratitude to him."

The server whizzed away on its squat wheeled base, swerving through the crowd which barely gave it a glance. Eve watched its erratic path, her thoughts so muddled she couldn't process, locked up like a computer with an overload of commands to process. She lost track of the server, but her gaze landed on a reedy man in unkempt khakis and a long brown overcoat. Not an unusual choice of clothing, except for the sheer fact the earthy tones stood out in the sea of black and metal.

Her heart seized. This must be MadDog.

She lifted her gaze to his face. Unattractive in a nondescript way, with greasy brown hair and a scraggly beard. Personal hygiene might not be a priority for him, but she didn't have to like him or date him. She only had to hand over the intel she carried so he could shout out to the world about Preditech's deception.

MadDog caught her stare, nodded once, and walked to the other side of the room, toward the restrooms and the alley exit. Eve clenched the edge of the table and drew in a deep breath.

This was it. Time to take down a corrupt corporation and save some cyborgs.

Chapter Three

dam watched Eve slide away from her table, the glass of wine he'd sent her untouched and forgotten. He followed the direction of her gaze to the cave troll in the brown coat. The guy had entered a few minutes ago, and Adam had known immediately this was MadDog. There was no way his meeting with Eve had romantic overtones. Opposites might attract, but no way classy-yet-secretive Eve would find anything about this this guy sexy, even if he had a dick the size of a wine bottle. True to his word, Adam had asked the guy if he was here to meet someone, and had received a snarly grunt in response which sounded every bit a *mind your own damn business.* So what was going on? Was he a distant relative? A long-lost brother? Was he her dealer? Had Adam misread her nervous behavior and she simply needed a fix?

If he was patient and cautious, he'd discover the truth, hopefully before the night went to hell. Dare he believe he could prevent the shit show from happening?

MadDog disappeared in the back hallway where the bathrooms and the storeroom doors intersected. Eve slowly followed in that direction, her focus intent on her destination. She bumbled against the tough crowd gathered for the band, thrashing and whiplashing to the harsh beat thrumming through each fiber and cell. Adam had turned his cybernetic hearing to its lowest level to withstand the auditory onslaught, so he couldn't hear what she said to her human obstacles and his lip-reading software was useless without seeing the entirety of her lips. Her head swiveled like windshield wipers, searching for… what? She wasn't being discreet, but no one seemed to notice.

Adam shoved off the wall where he normally stationed himself and moseyed in the direction both MadDog and Eve had gone. He caught his boss's attention and jerked his head, the understood signal for a bathroom break. Taking care to be casual yet move quickly to catch them in whatever surreptitious deal they were making, he slipped into the dark hallway. This early in the band's first set, everyone crowded the stage and the bathrooms were empty. A quick peek didn't reveal MadDog or Eve. Adam checked the door to the storeroom, but it was locked like normal.

Hands on his hips, he stood in the hall. If they'd exited into the alley, the alarms would have gone off. But he hadn't seen them return to the dance floor. He switched his eye to heat signature. Sure enough, the exit door had two faint handprints. He inspected the door, looking for proof of sabotage. There, up in the corner where the security wire ran from door to wall, a small circuit loop was clipped, circumventing the alarm without tripping it. If The Vogue's owner had listened to Adam's suggestions and upgraded the security system into the twenty-second century instead of depending on the city's street cameras which scanned alley entrances, this would never have happened. Perhaps this was why Eve and MadDog had chosen to meet here tonight.

Adam leaned his hip against the push bar and paused. What was he walking into? What if they were exchanging drugs? What if she was a pro and they were having sex? What if they were—he floundered for a worse scenario—doing interpretive dance?

A muffled scream sounded from the other side of the thick door. Adrenalin shot through Adam as he shoved open the door and burst into the alley. He skidded to a halt at the vision of MadDog in Eve's arms, his face between her breasts as she undulated against him. Disappointment joined the adrenalin. He was wrong about Eve. Wrong about her reason for meeting MadDog. He stepped back to go inside, but Eve turned her head toward him.

His retreat faltered. His muscles tensed and his cybernetic systems flipped to full alert.

Her eyes were wide, filled with fear and tears, not passion. Adam blinked. MadDog wasn't nuzzling her breasts, he was leaning against her, his body sliding downward as she struggled to hold him upright. He collapsed on the ground with a gurgled last breath, a trickle of bloody foam on his mouth. Eve sobbed, her arms out as if in supplication, a trail of red staining the front of her shirt. She met Adam's gaze again.

His blood buzzed in his veins. Wait. That wasn't his blood buzzing. He switched his hearing controls to high and caught the distinctive hum of a drone rising overhead. He switched to night vision and glanced skyward. The receding blip of a drone snagged his attention for a moment before it was out of sight. Government issue—military grade, judging by the outline against the night sky—and supposedly only used for stealth missions against terrorist leaders in foreign countries. This had been a hit.

"He jumped in front of me." Eve's hoarse whisper pulled Adam's gaze back to the dead body in the alley. He didn't need his cyborg senses to know Eve was in shock. She trembled, her face ashen and her eyes hollow. "That shot was meant for me."

Shit creek and no paddle. Adam would have to call the cops, and they would want to interview all the bar patrons, especially

Eve whom they'd consider a prime suspect. Echoing her own claim, Adam's gut said she'd been the target. If the owner of a government drone had tried to off her, police procedure would keep her exposed for an easy second attack. Every cell and synthetic fiber in his body agreed he had to keep her safe.

His predicament was almost humorous in its irony. Turns out he was going to go all rogue-robot tonight. Just not in dramatic building-smashing manner Hollywood depicted.

He reached in his front pocket and pulled out his car fob. Nodding toward it, he muttered loudly enough for her to hear. "I drive the black classic Mustang in the garage across the street, second level. There's a blanket in the back. Walk out the front door like you've done it a hundred times and find my car. If anyone stops you, you've been stood up for a blind date. Cover up and lay low until I get out of here."

She shook her head. "Thanks, but I'll wait and talk to the police."

An expected response, and he didn't blame her for it. But he had to dissuade her, for her own safety. "Normally, I'd advise the same. But if that shot had been meant for you, staying will only give whoever pulled the trigger a second chance at you. You're out of time and choices."

Her chest heaved with a shuddering breath as she processed his words. She nodded, clamped her suit jacket over her chest and stepped toward him, reaching for the key he offered. His fingers tingled where hers brushed against them. If it had been his left hand, he would worry it was glitching again. He had no excuse for what was happening to his right hand.

He cleared his throat. "Your phone."

She paused, staring at the back door. "He'd told me not to bring it." She croaked, hitching her purse strap on her shoulder, then hurried back into the building. The unnerving tingle in his fingers ceased.

Adam waited a couple minutes before calling 9-1-1 with his

internal communicator. If he was lucky, they'd send rookies who didn't know of him. But he wouldn't hold his breath. His luck rarely worked in his favor. This was going to be a long night filled with interrogation, suspicion, and condescension.

So, other than the dead body, just like old times.

Chapter Four

Eve shuddered and her body screamed to move, to run. Cowering in the back seat of Adam's car, covered in a flannel blanket on a warm summer night, trying to stay motionless so no one in the busy parking garage would notice her in the back seat did little to ease her fraught emotions. Her head hurt from the battle of thoughts and emotions raging in it. Fortunately, the garage was temperature-controlled, but she was still toasty. Little doubt her makeup had melted off and the blood on her shirt had transferred to the rest of her clothes, mixing with perspiration for a yicky, sticky stew that seeped into her bones. She'd never wash it all out.

Her contact was dead. Had died in her arms, blood oozing from his eyes and nose from whatever had hit him. They'd been making small talk, feeling each other out before the actual trade of info. She couldn't remember what innocuous comment she was making when MadDog had grabbed her and whipped them both around. He had flinched and grunted, his eyes rolling back in his head. He'd managed a strangled "they know" before his face had turned into a river of blood and he'd collapsed into her arms, foaming and convulsing.

She'd never had to deal with death before, not even that of a pet. She'd only ever known the peaceful, final pose which made a person look like they dressed up to take a nap. She certainly had no experience with this bloody, ugly, struggling kind of dying. And definitely not murder.

MadDog had sacrificed his life for her. Or at least for the information still taped behind her ear. Odd, because he didn't strike her as a self-sacrificing kind of guy. Maybe the whole thing had been a hoax to frighten her away and he wasn't dead. But she hadn't given him the information yet, so the hoax hadn't worked. And Adam either thought MadDog was dead, or he was also in on the charade.

Maybe they were messing with her to keep her from blowing the top off Preditech's deception. That could explain why Adam had miraculously appeared as MadDog crumpled to the ground. And her panic at experiencing someone dying in such an ugly, violent manner was the perfect opportunity to secure her trust and get her away from the crowd and into their clutches. But that was an overly elaborate prank to implement.

She should run away. She should find another person who could spread the information she carried. Or she should find the way to deliver it to the right sources so Preditech could no longer hide its crimes. Be the one to help make things right. She should—

Christ her head hurt! Too many questions without answers and actions without means. As much as her panicked flight response urged her muscles to action, something about the weight of the blanket kept her in place. Like a hug. And it smelled... nice. Manly. Like campfire and bourbon mixed with a slight metallic tang. An odd combination for someone who worked in a bar. She inhaled long, deep breaths to soothe her overworked nerves, letting the calm strength of the scent mixture fill her cells. The blanket and the car muffled the sounds of

Saturday night in Old Broad Ripple to a white noise which further lulled her agitation.

She'd been on edge for a couple weeks, researching and planning how to get the mini-drive into the right hands. Into hands which could make a difference. Always looking over her shoulder. Not knowing who to trust, not having a guide or connections or a clue on how and in what direction to proceed. Having watched her only contact possibly die in front of her. And the damn drive was still taped to her head, pulling and itching her scalp where beads of sweat formed.

But in the quiet warmth of Adam's car, under the soothing embrace of an old blanket, the worry and fear ebbed like low tide, still quietly within reach, but no longer surging against her.

She was a hot mess and her life was circling the drain. But for these past few hours, she could almost believe it was a dream. The murder attempt, the conspiracy, her lonely life… all of it was just a crazy, messed up dream and she'd soon wake up in the arms of a sexy, supportive, gentle man to greet her perfect, orderly life. Maybe that perfect man would wake her with sweet, passionate kisses—

The car door jerked open, yanking her from her fantasy, and someone plopped into the driver's seat before she could yelp. Something tapped on her, maybe his hand, searching for something.

"The key." He muttered, his voice further muffled by the blanket so she barely heard him. With as much stealth as her fraught nerves could muster, she reached the key to the edge of the material so he could grab it. "Now, don't move or say a word."

The car's engine rumbled to life, sounding like the growls of a feral cat, and they lumbered through the turns of the garage and onto the street, hiccupping and spitting along the way. He hadn't lied when he'd said his car was a classic. The need for an actual key fob was a dead giveaway, as were the worn seats and lack of an after-market driverless control panel. The Mustang model hadn't been manufactured for a several decades. Probably should be resting in a junkyard somewhere with the rest of its brethren, but was somehow still running. Or rather lurching, hacking, and backfiring down the streets like an elderly man past his prime but still too feisty to surrender.

"Come on, baby. Keep it together." Adam whispered. Eve's heart warmed at the endearment. "I'll change your oil next week. Just hang on."

Change her what? Oh, he was talking to the car. Eve's heart whined in tune with the rattling engine. Stupid to assume he'd meant the term for her. He'd known her for maybe five minutes, when he obviously had a long-term relationship with the vehicle. She was no expert, but would bet money on the fact an oil change would do little to help smooth out the ride. The Mustang needed some serious repair work. But what, she had no idea, and honestly, thinking about it was simply a distraction to her own problems. At least the air conditioning worked, and it's refreshing chill seeped through the blanket.

Several minutes passed as the car weaved around what little traffic there was at this late hour. She'd lost track of time, and Adam wasn't forthcoming with any information or small talk. If he was helping her, she didn't want to muck things up, and if he was plotting her demise, she didn't want to anger him. But she couldn't stand the silence. "Um, where are we going?"

She heard his exhausted sigh through the barrier of material. He answered in a low voice. "To my house, unless you have a better idea. Cops are all over the area, looking for a woman several patrons had seen following MadDog toward the back of The Vogue."

She gasped. Someone had watched her? "I didn't realize any of those kids had noticed me."

"Well, you do kinda stand out in a crowd."

At five-six, she was average height for a woman. So, he

probably meant she hadn't looked like the rest of the bar's clientele. She kicked herself for not trying harder to blend in with the band crowd, but she'd lacked the time to shop for a leather corset or studded leggings.

"Eve, did you drive or hire a ride?"

"My car drove from Chicago. It's in the lot three blocks east."

"Not to scare you, but I would venture a guess whoever tried to kill you is watching your car right now, hoping you'll come back for it. Let's give them some time to cool off, get bored, or maybe get recalled."

They slowed to a stop on a patch of crunchy gravel and a hum sounded nearby, like a small engine. The car proceeded for a short bit before stopping again, then a loud grinding sound which stopped with a solid clunk of wood and metal. Adam shut the car off and heaved a deep sigh. Silence blared and the summer heat began to seep in again.

Eve peeked out from beneath the blanket. Illuminated by one bare lightbulb shining through the car windows, Adam rubbed his eyes and scratched the scruff along his jawline, obviously exhausted. His voice was heavy with fatigue. "Give me a couple minutes to check my blinds are down and I don't have any dirty underwear lying around. Then you can come in."

He obviously spoke to her because he didn't call her *baby*. Without a glance her way, he heaved himself out of the car and closed the door, leaving her alone in her stifling oasis under the blanket. The muted sounds of Saturday night frivolity were long gone, and the silence blared.

Eve stabbed a guess at how long a couple minutes were before crawling out from her cozy nest. They were parked in a home garage. The humming, grinding sounds must have been the door lifting and lowering. She exited the car, the sultry heat at this late hour crowding out the remaining comfort from the car's air conditioning. August in Indiana was so much more oppressive than Chicago, which enjoyed the cooling effect of nearby Lake Michigan. But at least she wasn't under the blanket anymore.

The garage was filled with the expected smells of grease and oil and hints of that campfire-bourbon-metal aroma. Tools and canisters and half-finished electronic projects were scattered along benches and shelves lining the one-car room. If she could judge Adam's character by his car and garage alone, she'd say he was careless and inattentive. Maybe he subscribed to the philosophy that a messy workspace was a sign of genius, but Eve did not and so fought the urge to organize the mess. Or at least create a more direct path from the car to the door, instead of having to circumvent a fridge which jutted at odd angles from where it had been shoehorned against the wall and the steps.

"Dear god, this is the stuff of horror movies." She wrapped her jacket more tightly around her body, afraid to get any lingering grease or other garage-y substances on it. Which was silly, right? After all, she already had blood and sweat on the thing.

Eve paused at the thought as she opened the door. She closed her eyes and swallowed back her nausea at the night's events. Forget organizing Adam's garage, she needed to fix her own life first. She rubbed her lips together, searching for words which might help her achieve that goal and finding only the recent wisdom of a certain bar bouncer. "Come on, baby. Keep it together."

Crash! The sound came from inside the house, followed by a growled "Fuck!"

Chapter Five

Adam plunked the cabinet door onto the counter. His damn malfunctioning hand still gripping the handle, the wooden square a splintered carcass where his cybernetic arm had snapped it from its frame on an uncontrolled flex.

Thank the Maker he'd opted to get a glass first, or else he'd be holding his fridge door instead, and his beer and leftover pizza would get warm.

Eve ran into the kitchen, her eyes wide with alarm. "Are you okay? What happened? Why is your cabinet door ripped off its hinges?"

He held up a hand to calm her frantic stream of questions, and divert her attention from the broken door his hand refused to release. "Last of the safety checks, and the thing fell off. Serves me right for buying a fixer-upper instead of a new home."

Yeah, like he would ever buy a house built after the turn of the twenty-second century. He almost snorted in disdain. Who knew what sort of government *oversight* got planted into new construction under the auspices of safety. And who knew how it might affect his cyborg parts. With his luck, he'd smack himself in the head every time he flushed the toilet.

She wrapped her arms around her stomach, a classic move for someone feeling exposed. Glancing around at what she could see of his home, her tone suggested she didn't believe his excuse. "Did you think an intruder might be hiding in the cabinet? Or a stray pair of underpants?"

He forced a chuckle and turned to the cabinet as if to inspect the damage, silently willing his unresponsive hand to let go and praying his arm wouldn't flinch wildly again. "Hey, it's a bachelor pad. Weirder things are possible."

Sending her what he hoped was a casual glance over his shoulder, Adam nodded toward the rest of the house. "Look, it's late. Why don't you get some sleep? Bedroom's to the right, down the hall, and the door locks. The sheets aren't exactly fresh, but throw a blanket on them. Help yourself to whatever shirts are in the dresser, just ignore the *Playboys* in the bottom drawer."

Her eyebrows screwed into a knot. "What are play boys?"

His bark of laughter was as hollow as his mechanical heart. He turned back to the counter, wrestling his fingers out of the door handle and shaking his head. Was he such an antique a woman nearly his own age knew nothing about the things he considered classic? "If you don't know, you should definitely avoid the bottom drawer."

He wiggled the fingers, finally relaxed enough to release the door handle, and turned back to Eve. "Don't worry, they won't attack you."

Damn. Bad choice of words. Her face fell, and fear crept into her expression. She shivered and hugged her body more tightly. "Is that what happened in the alley? What did the police say? Shouldn't I go make a statement or something?"

She looked lost, her haunted eyes on him as if he had all the answers. Three hours of *real* cops crawling over the crime scene and interviewing angry, belligerent bar patrons as Adam tried to act innocent while eavesdropping on as many conversations as he could, and he didn't know much more than he had when he'd followed her to the alley. He knew more than the cops, but he wasn't about to admit he'd heard a state-of-the-art drone over-head. If he had, he would also have had to explain how he'd seen a drone, why no one else had seen it, and how he'd determined it was military issue. He would have had to explain who the hell he thought he was trying to be more than a bar bouncer and who'd gone and made him a detective.

His gut told him to keep his cards close to the chest. If he advertised what he knew, the information wouldn't help keep Eve safe or find her killer.

Adam stepped toward her, his fingers itching to sooth the frown line between her brows. Since those same fingers had helped rip off a cabinet door, he wasn't about to give in to the urge to touch Eve. Visions of her head clutched in his rogue hand while her lifeless body collapsed to the floor kept him from the temptation she posed. "You don't want to talk to the police. They'll assume you're the culprit."

"Culprit? I was almost the victim!" Indignation replaced fear. Good, because he lacked the bedside manner to deal with fear.

"Victim of what crime? Committed by who? What proof do you have? You were alone in the alley with the now-dead-guy so you have no one to corroborate your story, which means you could be making up the whole thing. And since you planned to meet him, it would be considered pre-meditated."

"But you saw. You can corroborate."

He didn't dare tell her the police would suspect her more if he stood up for her. "They wouldn't consider me a trustworthy witness. Besides, I only saw a man die in your arms, not how he died or who did it."

With each statement, her face fell and tears shimmered in her eyes. "M-maybe he didn't actually die?"

Her voice was soft and high, like a lost little girl. He was an ass for being so antagonistic. He sighed and stepped to her, his left hand grabbing the back of his belt so if it glitched, his body and not hers would receive the damage. He slowly lifted his right hand to gently squeeze her shoulder. He had never been good at offering comfort, leaving that to other cops and opting for the bad-cop role during interrogations. "I wish that were the case, but we both watched him die. The EMT confirmed it. Look, Eve, you're here because I believe you and I want to keep you safe until we find out who did this."

Had he really said *we?* When had he decided to help her?

She sniffed, raising a hopeful gaze to his. He could drown in the warm depths of those eyes, which answered his unspoken question about *when.* Her lips hitched upward on one side. "Thank you."

If she'd said anything else, Adam might have claimed those pink lips in a kiss because—damn it all to hell—it had been a long time since he'd been with a woman, especially one as beautiful as Eve, and her smile was a welcome wagon he wanted to board. But she'd gone and thanked him. Been grateful for what had mostly been him selfishly saving his own ass from more hassle than absolutely necessary. He looked at the dingy tile of his kitchen floor and scrubbed a safe hand through his hair. "Don't thank me. You haven't slept in my bed or eaten my cooking yet. Jail might look pretty good by comparison."

"Nonsense." Her smile hit full wattage, and his lungs malfunctioned, refusing to draw in air. Weird, because they weren't cybernetic. She stepped forward and planted a peck on his cheek, then pulled back. "Your accommodations come with freedom and possibility. Jail doesn't."

She flounced toward the back of the house, confident footsteps finding his bedroom and closing the door. His cheek still tingled from the contact of her lips. He touched the spot with his mechanical fingers, surprised that for at least one moment, he didn't worry he might malfunction and either die or hurt someone. Truth be told, having another person in his home was kind of nice. It had been a long time for that as well. If he could keep his distance, and her away from his *Playboys*, this might work out.

"What are you getting yourself into, Lemon?" He shook his head, grabbed a beer from the fridge using his right hand, and walked to the cluttered office space in the corner of his living room. He had several questions, beginning with who the hell this MadDog had been.

Chapter Six

S afely ensconced in Adam's sparse bedroom, Eve sat on the edge of his bed and opened the floodgate to her emotions. Sobs bent her over until she was nearly fetal, tears pouring through her fingers and onto the skirt of her suit. She cried all the thoughts from her brain and emotion from her heart. Cried until her throat was sore and her fingers wrinkled.

How had tonight gone so wrong? How had her plans to do the right thing swerved and imploded so intensely? One minute, she's trying to save cyborgs, and the next she's holding the convulsing body of a dying man.

Where did this leave her, besides in the bedroom of a bar bouncer who'd been kind enough to get her away from the scene of the murder-meant-for-her? Fate was a tumultuous ocean, and she sailed a small, rudderless craft with no life vest, clinging to the sides and hoping it didn't capsize. Eve wiped her face, her skin tight and itchy from the salt of her many tears. She wasn't going to save the world if she didn't pull herself together. The only way to tackle the situation was one step at a time. Line by line in a spreadsheet, like how she approached her work projects.

She blinked away the last of her spent heartache and looked

around Adam's bedroom. It was tidy, all dirty clothes located in the hamper and the top sheet and coverlet pulled up to the pillows. Maybe this was how he lived, or maybe this was a result of the few minutes he'd had before she entered his home, but she was relieved he wasn't a complete slob.

His furniture was solid wood, if well-used and mismatched. The same for the fabrics, his curtains and bedspread faded navy patterns. If he'd ever had a woman in his life, it had been a long time ago and she'd had little decorating style. The knowledge was oddly comforting.

His single dresser had a worn comb and a small brass dish with dusty coins on its top. No pictures. Three doors: one to the hall, one for a tiny closet, and the other a bathroom barely larger than the closet which contained the same minimal simplicity. A dingy shower curtain, unassuming toiletries, and faded bath towels. Nothing that hinted at any sort of vanity or self-pampering. He either had no one in his life to impress, or he didn't care. If the way he looked was the result of his not caring, Eve wasn't sure whether to be grateful for his natural mouth-watering appeal, or angry it distracted her from what she needed to do.

She eased the top dresser drawer open, her curiosity growing about the handsome man in the other room who seemed to live a plain and solitary life. The drawer was filled with sloppy stacks of shirts in hues one might consider the opposite of color. Black, charcoal, gray. Not a rich brown, forest green, or deep plum, which was a shame because he would look amazing in those colors. She rummaged through the stack, and pulled out a random T-shirt. The second drawer held a mish-mash of jeans and sweats, so she grabbed a pair of sweats with a drawstring waistband. Curiosity getting the better of her, she ignored his previous warning and opened the bottom drawer. Amid dark socks—no underwear, which was all kinds of titillating—rested several paper magazines in the same shape as the rest of his home: old, worn, and faded.

She lifted the top one from the drawer and cradled the delicate issue in her hands. Paper was so rare these days, a sense of reverence washed over her. She held history in her hands. The cover of these sacred pages showed a naked young woman, her back arched and her expression a soft invitation. Full lips slightly parted, her doe eyes heavy with desire. Her lithe arms lifted and entangled in her hair, leaving her full, firm breasts exposed. The pages were yellowed, but full of text broken occasionally by pictures of other nubile women in states of undress. The publish date was nearly half a century ago, if the makeup and hairstyles of the nude models weren't enough to prove this magazine was an antique.

Her grandfather sometimes talked about such gentlemen's publications. Her grandmother had huffed in exasperation when he had, but apparently these magazines had once been a bastion of information for men, offering articles and stories and instructions such as the "How to give her Multiple Orgasms" this one boasted. Why had Adam not wanted her to see these? Was this supposed to be a secret? Were women not supposed to know about these? Glancing through the pages, the photography was something along the lines of artistic nudes. If the pictures of beautiful women and a few ribald cartoons was the incentive men needed to read, that wasn't so bad. It wasn't anything he should feel compelled to keep hidden from her.

Finding his magazines answered one of the many Adam riddles bouncing in her brain, already filled with questions and worries and emotions struggling for attention. Exhaustion swept over her and she quickly changed out of her work day suit and into her pilfered clothes, the shirt hanging on her slender frame, so unlike the voluptuous young women in the *Playboy*. She folded her clothes neatly, set them on the floor by the nightstand, and climbed into his bed atop the comforter. Rolling to her side, she took an edge with her, making an Eve enchilada.

Five minutes ago, she would have denied being able to fall

asleep, her nerves too overwrought to unwind. But in his surprisingly comfortable bed, surrounded by the scent she had already come to assume was all Adam—campfire, bourbon, and that hint of metal—her muscles turned to jelly. The tension and stress of the past couple weeks drained away and a kernel of actual hope flickered in her chest. She shouldn't trust Adam, but wrapped in the warmth and safety of his bedsheets, her objections drifted away as sleep claimed her. How warm and safe would she be wrapped in his arms?

Chapter Seven

Adam rubbed his eyes, crusty and irritated from staring at his computer screen during the early morning hours. He could have saved his eyes serious strain by doing the internet search scroll internally through his micro-processor. In spite of his cybernetic enhancements, he was old-fashioned at best. Sometimes having the physical distance of a computer screen gave perspective the inside of his head couldn't provide. Not that perspective was good news in this situation.

Turned out MadDog wasn't named for a cheap alcohol. He was an internet blogger known for breaking out information many didn't want public. A whistleblower. He'd gotten his reputation during the Leviathan trials a dozen years ago when he'd rabidly insisted there was a third party pulling the strings. He'd been right. Or crazy, depending on which news channel you read.

Regardless, why had Eve met him in the alley behind The Vogue? MadDog only dealt in the currency of information. Since Eve had been the target, she was likely the person with the information. If they hadn't completed the transaction, Eve would still be a target. Which begged the question, what kind of information did she have that would put her in the crosshairs of a government drone. He could use his interrogation skills to extract the answer from her, but that was harsh. And if he knew what she knew, he'd also be a target—

Stupid fuck, he was already a target by the sheer fact he'd given her refuge for the night. If he'd wanted to play it safe, he should have left her in the alley. Hell, he should never have followed her there in the first place. If he kicked her to the curb, he'd still be considered a secondary target. He had to continue along the path he'd chosen. He had to help her.

While finding MadDog's identity had been relatively easy, Adam had been forced to dig much deeper for his second question: what had killed MadDog?

He'd been oozing blood and frothing at the mouth. Whatever he'd been hit with had been fast-acting and easy to administer from a distance with little more than a simple projectile the size of a pinky nail. Even government drones lacked the heft for major ballistic weaponry, and Adam had spied through his magnification lens the tiny dart embedded in MadDog's neck while the police had conducted their crime scene investigation.

To find answers, Adam had to dig past the typical medical sites which claimed the symptoms were cancer. He eventually landed on some looney conspiracy theorists speculating a government-supported dabbling in viral warfare, including a genetically manipulated combination of Ebola and Marburg viruses, known tentatively as TC-14.

Adam swallowed back a lump of fear. And the world believed *cyborgs* were a scary threat.

"Did you get any sleep?" Her soft inquiry came from the arched doorway. He swiveled to face her, his lungs seizing again and his brain blanking. Oh, but his zombie cock perked awake. She leaned against the door frame, dressed in one of his shirts, its hem skimming thighs barely covered by a thin pair of sweats. The collar dangled off one unadorned shoulder, and it was the sexiest thing he'd seen in a decade. She hugged her midriff, which bunched her breasts together. She was long and lean and her breasts were a mere palmful. But to a starving man, they were a feast on a platter. He'd never been so jealous of an article of clothing before, and his rousing penis surged to attention.

Adam scrubbed a hand over his face, willing the randy member back to sleep. "I dozed off a little, but I'm used to running on fumes."

"Not to sound like your mother, but that's not very healthy." She finger-combed her sleep-tangled hair and wandered into the room, sitting on a dated leather footstool and folding her legs primly at an angle. Aside from her shoulder and forearms, the only other flesh he spied was two slender ankles and ten dainty toes. And damn if that wasn't sexier than any of the naked women in his old *Playboys* or splayed across the online porn sites.

He cleared his throat and pulled his mind out of the gutter. "Trust me, you don't sound anything like my mother."

A slow smile spread across her lips and her eyelids dipped for a few heartbeats, as if he'd complimented her. Was that a good thing or a bad thing? If she reacted like this from a simple statement of truth, what would she do if he applied the effort to compliment her beauty?

"Sooooo." She drew the word out. Combined with how she mashed her lips together at the end, she was working up the nerve to ask him something. As her subtle floral scent threatened to short-circuit his wiring, he leaned back in his chair and tried to act casual and nonthreatening until she finally asked her question. "What were you doing instead of sleeping?"

A hundred responses tumbled through his brain, but he needed to secure her trust and honesty. A little tit for tat was in order, and he sternly reminded his dick the *tit* wasn't her chest. The truth came forth easily. "I was searching for information about MadDog."

The blood drained from her face. Was she thinking about her

near-murder? Was she worried he'd learned whatever secret she had? "There's no news about his death." Adam assured her.

She didn't look assured. "What does that signify?"

He tilted his head to catch her gaze. "It depends. Either the police haven't yet processed the paperwork for the news media to catch and report, or someone is keeping a lid on the news."

Her color returned. "But why? Why would anyone want to keep his death a secret?"

"You mean, why would anyone want to keep his *murder* a secret?"

Her color drained again. She was going to pass out from low blood pressure if he wasn't careful. She pulled her legs to her chest and hugged them, her slender fingers fiddling with the hem of the shirt she wore. "You mean, why would anyone want to keep the attempted murder of me a secret."

Her voice was small and frail, like last night. The need to pull her into his arms and promise her everything would be okay was strong, nearly overriding his sense of survival and need to keep his own secrets. He leaned toward her, elbows on his knees, modulating his voice like one might do with a frightened child or frenzied pet. Or flight-risk criminal. "Eve, why were you meeting MadDog last night? Why do you know him? Why would anyone want to kill you?"

She met his gaze and nibbled on her lips, obviously determining how little she could confess. He tried to nip that line of thinking. "I can't help you if I don't know anything."

"I... um. I have a..." She chuffed her hands along her upper arms for warmth. "I know things."

He paused and waited for her to put her thoughts together. She drew in a deep breath. "Can I just admit I have some information I shouldn't have? Is that enough?"

Didn't give him much to go on. "What kind of information? Winning lottery numbers? Bank security codes? Access passwords to nuclear launch systems?"

"Um… Corporate corruption?"

He shrugged. "Are we talking Big Pharma? Energy? Coffee? No news with any of those."

She chuckled softly. "No, different industry. And it's not inflated stock prices or customers being overcharged. These customers are being killed."

Her eyes bugged and her face turned white again. She'd said more than she'd meant to. Before he could say something to assure her confidence, she dropped her head into her hands. "You're bad for my self-preservation."

Her tone lacked any severe accusation. He scanned her and detected no rise in temperature, but her heartrate had increased, which could mean anything. Nerves, anger, arousal. Without knowing the source, he couldn't gauge how to react. Honestly, he was too tired do much of anything at this point. He stood and scratched the seven-am shadow on his jawline. "Look, I need a nap. Thirty minutes tops. After that, we'll go grab some food and get your car."

"I'm sorry for being such a burden." She popped to a stand and hugged her torso again. She was either a masterful seductress or was oblivious to what a sensual morning-after vision she presented. Whichever the case, Adam would have a difficult time falling asleep with that mental image, no matter that he was exhausted. She toed the short shag of his beige carpet. "I appreciate everything you've done for me and don't want to intrude any more than I already have. Let me change clothes and I'll get out of your hair."

Adam waved away her objection. "Eve, you are free to leave whenever you like, but you're not a burden. I'm already involved by my own free will, and if someone is truly trying to kill you, going out alone is a surefire way to give them the chance to do that."

She drew in a shuddering breath and nodded. Tears shimmered at the edges of her eyes when she finally lifted her gaze to his. She sniffed and swallowed hard. "I don't want to put you in danger—"

"I already am. And knew I would be the moment I gave you my car fob."

"Adam, I… I wish I could do this by myself, but I can't. Thank you. Go, sleep as long as you need to. I'll entertain myself and try not to get into trouble."

Adam showed her the menu screen for his old holo-projection TV and apologized for only knowing the sports channels. The downside of preferring old-school options. He invited her to make herself at home, tried to ignore the pile of her clothes on his bedroom floor, and sat on the edge of his bed, scrubbing a hand down his face and feeling older than his years. What the hell had he gotten into? Not the part about saving Eve from possible murder and a certain trip to jail, but about bringing her to his house. There were reasons he lived alone, and he could count those reasons on one arm. One glitching cyborg arm which could be more dangerous to Eve's life than a government-issued drone.

Do you trust me, Adam?

Dr. Farrow's words drifted from the depths of his memory. The tolerant and understanding rehabilitation doctor who had helped Adam in the early days after his surgery. Helped him work through the pain and the adjustment, until his enhancements worked in tandem with the rest of his body instead of against. At a time when everyone else in his life had left him, Doc had stood beside him, encouraging him, believing in him.

When Adam could function on his own, he'd done to Doc what everyone else had done to him: walked away without so much as a *thank you* or *go to hell*.

So why did Doc's mantra come forward now? Nearly eight years after Adam had decided he no longer needed the man's help, the oft-uttered conversation rolled over him like a shot of whiskey.

Do you trust me, Adam?

This was the question the doctor had often asked him, especially in those frustrated moments when rehabilitation had seemed impossible.

Yeah, Doc. I trust you. I just don't trust myself.

Then you'll have to trust me when I say you will find your way through this.

Find his way through harboring a beautiful woman and keeping her safe, not only from whoever wanted her dead but also from himself, while he lusted after her like a convict who'd been in solitary for years?

He'd found his way through the pain of his enhancement surgery. Had found a way to scrape out a life of his own. Had found a way through the heartache of being discarded—okay, had *almost* found a way through the heartache. Maybe Doc was right. He would find a way to keep Eve safe from whoever was after her. And keep her safe from him by keeping her at arm's length.

Although he'd much rather keep her safe within the circle of his arms.

Weary to the bone, he laid down without crawling under the covers. Big mistake. His comforter smelled of her. Flowers and sunny spring mornings. Hope and possibility. He turned his face to the fabric and filled his lungs with it. God he could drown in her scent. It called to a deep, long-buried part of him. A part he didn't want roused. Like how he didn't want his dick roused either. Yet here he sported a tent pole. He should lock himself in the bathroom and take quick care of it. He should maybe take an overdue shower, clean off last night's work shift, and jack his throbbing attraction to Eve out of his system. He *shouldn't* turn further into the comforter and release his erection from the constriction of his pants, much less snuffle Eve's aroma and imagine his hand was hers until he moaned out his climax onto the sheets.

But he did. Afterward, he wiped the mess with tissue like he was back in high school trying to hide the evidence from his parents.

Fortunately, he didn't have the energy to be embarrassed about any of it. And when he fastened his jeans and rolled back onto the bed, he dropped immediately into a deep, dreamless sleep.

Chapter Eight

Eve didn't do idle well, and watching television smacked of laziness. Instead, she wandered the small house. The short-pile dirty-beige carpet muffled her steps so she didn't wake Adam. She steered clear of the bedroom hallway, afraid the pull to sneak a peek of him sleeping, and maybe curl up against his muscled form, would prove too difficult to resist.

After a few minutes memorizing the layout of the home and peering out the covered windows at the quaint neighborhood of older, but maintained ranch-style homes with tidy lawns awash in slanted bands of bright morning sunlight, she sat at his computer and tinkered around the internet. Meaning she searched for news about herself, Preditech, and MadDog. She needed to know what information was out there and who might be looking for her. And more importantly, she needed a new contact to whom she could give the mini-drive. She'd transferred it from her hairline to under her breast, and it weighed heavily on that rib like she'd taped a brick instead.

The internet held no helpful information. As far as the real world was concerned, a television network's upcoming cyborg hunter series was the biggest news out there. Eve almost laughed in bitter realization no one knew what she knew, which meant no one would know she was trying to save lives. Not that she had any delusions of grandeur, but no one would know to appreciate the sacrifice she was making. They would continue their lives in blissful ignorance, unaware of the monstrous neglect Preditech had chosen.

Still, she would persevere. Someone had to do something, or people would continue to die. Her conscience would not rest until she'd done everything possible to help right those wrongs. Would Adam think she was doing the right thing, or would he think she was crazy? Would he turn his back on her for being a cyborg sympathizer? Did she dare find out?

No, she wasn't brave enough to risk seeing the horror or derision on his face. She much preferred his confident swagger and kindness. If only she could thank him another way besides verbally. Sleeping with him popped into her brain as an option, but she rejected the idea. Offering sexual favors was too much out of character for her, and although the idea of a hot fuck with the sexy bouncer was a fantasy she'd save for those lonely nights once her life returned to normal, she didn't look anything like the young, voluptuous nudes in his magazines. She wasn't his type.

But she could offer the next best thing: a good meal.

Eve beelined to the kitchen. The coffee supplies were easy enough to locate and soon she had a pot brewed to scalding perfection. The actual meal was a bit trickier. Adam was either at the tail end of a paycheck or preferred take-out. Only a few cans of Sun King Wee Mac, a local micro-brew beer if she's read the label correctly, populated the fridge. A couple shriveled slices of meat pizza rested in their cardboard box and a few lonely eggs huddled in the door. She plucked them up, hoping they weren't too old, and rummaged through the cabinets and found half a box of spaghetti, garlic powder, chili flakes, and a nearly-empty jar of roasted peanuts. A random mix of ingredients for sure, and not enough to make a fabulous meal. But she could cobble together an edible Pad Thai.

"I can fix this." She nodded and spoke to the room, energized by having direction and purpose. So caught up in cooking, she nearly dropped the pan on a yelp when Adam entered and poured a mug of coffee.

"Smells like food in here." His voice was deeper and rougher with sleep, and a shiver ran the length of her spine. He leaned against the counter, wearing only a low-slung pair of dark jeans and running a hand through his damp hair. He'd taken a shower, and damn if that didn't conjure a wealth of mouth-watering images. Colorful dual sleeve tattoos ran the length of his arms and spilled over his shoulders, stopping where his patch of silvery chest hair blossomed like a firework, and dwindled to a darker line down his torso and dipped below the waistband of his pants.

Eve stared at the patch of hair, and the sizable bulge behind the denim material of his pants. Her hunger ratcheted a notch, a ravenous need which had nothing to do with her Pad Thai.

Adam stepped away from the counter and cleared his throat. "I mean, it smells good. What you cooked. Better than anything I ever make."

His movement jerked her back to the present. She stood in the middle of the kitchen, pan in one hand and spatula in another like she was going into battle, staring at the crotch of a stranger.

"I'm hungry." She shook her head, willing her brain to work again, her face aflame from the Freudian slip of her tongue. "I mean, I figured you were hungry. It's the best I could do, and it's not great. But it's okay. I hope you don't mind I picked through your pizza and pulled off the meat to add in."

She was rambling. She'd kick herself if she could. Instead, she scraped the contents of the pan onto a plate and set the plate on the small but sturdy kitchen table as he sat. Transferring the dirty dishes to the sink, she poured a cup of coffee. If only she had a little dribble of cream to soften the rich brew. More importantly, if only she could stop thinking about the half-dressed hottie behind her and how much she wanted him undressed.

"You're not eating?" His question surprised her and she did yelp, bobbling the mug but not spilling any as she faced him. He sat, the food untouched, gazing calmly at her like he did this every day.

"Uh… um, there's only enough for one. You eat. I'll be fine."

Her traitorous stomach took that moment to rumble loudly in the quiet room. Adam smiled in triumph and divided the Pad Thai on his plate while she pulled one from the cabinet and settled across from him. His knees brushed hers under the table as he scraped half of his noodle mixture onto her plate, and her body warmed from the innocent contact.

They ate in silence for a few bites. The dish was palatable in a strange fusion-cuisine way.

"This is good. Thank you for cooking."

She snorted. "You're being too kind, but you're welcome. It was the least I could do for as nice as you've been to me."

It was his turn to snort. "It's better than anything I could cook. And would it make you feel better to know I'm being purely selfish in helping you?"

She lifted an eyebrow at him. "Selfish? I'm not buying it."

He shrugged, twirling his fork in the noodles. He had a workingman's hands, thick and strong and weathered. His morning scruff emphasized the strong angle of his jawline, and a lock of salt-n-pepper hair slid down a forehead marred only by the creases that time and responsibility carved into it. So many men in her corporate world fought against the effects of aging, but Adam was a man who took it in stride. Like a mountain or a majestic oak tree. She wanted to lean against his strength.

"Yeah, selfish. I didn't want to have to deal with being fingered as an accomplice, having to take off work to show up for a trial, being questioned on the stand, having my past plastered all over the news."

That made sense. Judging by his muscular build, tattoos, and RSF—resting scowl face—he looked like someone whose past involved questionable decisions and run-ins with the police. But who was she to judge? She'd made her own share of stupid choices throughout her life. Her ex being one of them. Her blind loyalty to her employer being another.

Although her bad decisions only made her pathetic. Adam's made him exciting and sexy.

He cleared his throat. "Plus, I get to have a beautiful woman make me a meal. Watch out, or I might come up with reasons to keep you here."

He thought she was beautiful? He wanted to keep her around? Her heart stumbled, then galloped. These days, the men in her life only wanted cash flow statements from her. Even so, her physical reaction was out of proportion to Adam's words. He probably said that to every woman. The fact he'd brought her to his home didn't mean he wanted her to stay. She had someone trying to kill her, after all, and any man was bound to get tired of that drama.

"Sorry, that sounded a lot less creepy in my head." Adam sighed and shifted in his chair. "Trust me, I'm not a stalker kind of guy. It's just... it's been awhile since I've tried to..." He grimaced. "To make a good impression on someone."

Show up shirtless. Eve clamped her lips to keep that tidbit to herself. If he was simply being nice, it would make things awkward. Like way more awkward than they already were. She scooted a noodle around her plate and worried her lips together. "No need to apologize. It's been a long time since anyone's put forth the effort to impress me."

"No boyfriend? Girlfriend? Kids?"

Eve opened her mouth to answer but closed it. Would she be wise to tell Adam how little of a life she had in Chicago? How no one but a few coworkers would miss her if she went… missing? She cleared her throat. "No. I never wanted kids, a fact my selfish husband—*Ex*-husband—always appreciated."

The Pad Thai remnants on her plate were fascinating, and she stared at them, afraid to see how pitiful her admission was in his eyes. A cool, hard fingertip forced her chin up so she had to look at him. His eyes held only warmth and understanding.

"*Ex* is the best title for selfish husbands." He pulled his hand away like she'd bitten it, and tucked it across his torso. As if embarrassed by his own words he shoved a forkful of noodles into his mouth. But he didn't break eye contact.

"Better would be to not have married him in the first place."

Adam nodded. "Can't change the past, so beating yourself up about it is pretty useless. Best we can do is hope we don't repeat the mistakes." He dipped his head and laughed, a rough hitch like his throat had forgotten how to make the sound. "Sorry. That was pretty corny."

"No. You sounded like you speak from experience. Do you have a selfish ex, too?"

Adam stared at a point over her shoulder, maybe at the bent hardware of the broken cabinet door. Did he regret inviting a nosy woman into his home? The barely audible sounds of a world going about its Sunday business outside the house filtered into their little scene, a reminder they weren't as alone. That there was some normalcy of life out there, even if her own was circling the drain. Her heart beat in time to the soft ticking of an antique analog clock somewhere in the house.

Finally he heaved a deep sigh and looked back to his noodles. "Ex fiancée, yes. But I wouldn't call her selfish. Just… I guess, smart. Smarter than me, for sure."

A lifetime of self-recrimination filled the short statement. "Adam, don't let anyone tell you that because you're a bouncer at a bar—"

He shook his head to stop her words. Had he meant something else? "Years ago, I made a choice I thought would save me. It did, but only in the narrowest definition of that word."

With that, he shoved the last of the noodles in his mouth and stood, taking both their plates to the sink, effectively ending their conversation. He turned and leaned against the edge of the counter, his legs crossed at the ankle. "Take a shower if you like. We'll go get your car and—"

Knock. Knock. Knock.

Chapter Nine

Adam tensed at the sharp rap on his front door. He didn't have friends or family to stop by unannounced and he wasn't expecting any package deliveries. A random visitor this soon after what happened last night wasn't a coincidence. This couldn't be good.

"Stay right there and don't make a sound." He ordered under his breath as he exited the kitchen. Eve was pale, her eyes saucers of fear. He didn't have time to assure her or tell her to hide before another round of knocks echoed in the silent house.

The front door opened to the left, and Adam prayed he didn't rip it off its hinges like he had his cabinet. With every bit of concentration he could divert from awareness of the terrified woman in his kitchen, he pulled the door open enough to peek out and see the officer on his doorstep. Not just any officer. His old partner.

"Lose a bet, Grady?" Adam stepped outside and closed the door behind him. He leaned back against the solid wood and tucked his hands into his back pockets. Demeanor was crucial. While he hadn't done anything wrong, the law would consider his guest a person of interest and his actions to keep her safe as harboring and abetting. Anything smacking of guilt would be amplified into proof. "Or did you come to reminisce about the good ol' days?"

Damn, his bitterness came out. Well, better than guilt.

Grady had the grace to look sheepish. He rocked back on his heels, his paunch straining the buttons on his shirt. He'd opted for a clean-shaven scalp in light of his receding hairline, the shiny dome reflecting the morning sun. The day's heat and humidity hadn't hit full swing yet, but his ruddy face glistened with a sheen of perspiration. A quick thermal scan proved he was nervous. What the scan couldn't tell is why. Chances were likely Grady worried Adam would go rogue, and neither gun nor ballistics vest would help him if that were the case.

"Good to see ya, Lehmann." Grady's voice didn't match his words. "You seem to be doing okay for yourself."

Adam looked around at the crumbling concrete front porch and the patches he'd poured last year. The bushes along the front of his house which he swore he'd trimmed last week but were sprawling monsters of overgrowth. The front yard which was three days into desperately needing cut. "Guess so. I'm still here."

Grady rubbed his shiny pate. "Look, the Chief thought it would be best to send a friendly face to come talk to ya."

Adam swallowed the bitter laugh choking him. "You're a friendly face?"

"Sure. I mean. We were partners once. Went through a lot together, me and you."

"Up until we didn't." Adam's voice was tight, his teeth clenched. Fortunately, his fists were hidden in his back pockets, or Grady might take it as an aggressive gesture.

"Look, it could have as easily been me who got shot up. I coulda been the one on the gurney having to choose between life or death."

Anguish washed over Adam, like he was reliving *that* day

again. That day, when he and Grady had answered a routine domestic dispute call. Adam had rushed into the room, glancing over the bruised and beaten woman as he swept the scene, but the shot got to him first. Three, shots, to be exact. Three lucky shots which tore through him sideways, where his ballistics vest didn't cover. At the time, he'd only been aware of pain exploding through his body, which he'd later learned had been bullets shattering his arm, passing through to his heart, and another through his temple to his eyeball. He'd heard screams, maybe his own, as he crumpled to the ground. He had vague memories of sirens and people yelling, of feeling the cold fingers of death creep up his body, of agreeing to an experimental surgery to save his life. He also remembered waking to looks of horror from his fiancée and friends, and a physical torment beyond anything he'd ever known.

He'd worked through the physical pain during rehabilitation with Dr. Farrow. But the emotional ache was still raw.

"Yeah, Grady. You could have been the one having to choose, but you weren't." His voice was hard as steel, years of resentment pouring forth in spite of his efforts to stem the flow.

"I can't fault you for wanting to live."

"Maybe. But others did and you let them. Or were you too overwhelmed with survivor's guilt to stand up for your partner when everyone looked at me like I was a newly-minted Darth Vader."

That wound would never heal. He hated the snarling, injured beast inside him which wanted to lash out, wanted Grady to know the same misery. All these years, yearning to get back the only thing which had given him purpose and meaning. The life that had been ripped away from him. He'd chosen to live, and people who had claimed to love him had reacted like he should have done them a favor and chosen death. In essence he had, because his existence the last decade had been little more than a drab, empty coffin of trying to hide what he was while waiting for his body to figure out what his brain had known for a long time: he wasn't fit to live.

Adam stewed in his riled anger, waiting for Grady to pretend to apologize for the past. The other man opened and closed his mouth a couple times, no words coming forth to ease or incite the tension between them, the palpable rage which fairly shook Adam to the bones. He noted Grady's sagging jowls, his gin blossom nose, his stooped shoulders... His former partner looked less like the plucky officer he'd known while on the force and more like his own father months before he'd died twenty years ago. Adam had no delusion he was a spring chicken, but even with his malfunctioning parts, he didn't feel as old as Grady looked.

The rage died under the wet blanket of that thought. Might as well get on with what little life they both had left.

He sighed long and deep, settling on the top step of his pint-sized front stoop. "Sarg didn't send you to make amends. Why are you here?"

Grady shoved his hands in his pockets and jingled some change. He rocked back on his heels a couple times. "I'm supposed to bring you in for questioning about last night's murder."

Adam shrugged, trying to appear nonchalant. "Why? I answered hours of questions last night. Has there been a new development?"

"You know I can't talk to you about an ongoing investigation."

"Ah. So you get to ask questions and I don't."

"You work at a bar, Lehmann. You know you don't have the authority anymore."

"You're right. I'm just a dumb bouncer. Which means I don't know anything else that I haven't already told three of the city's finest. I'm tired and I have another long shift in a few hours. So do we have to do this? Now?"

Grady rocked on his heels again. Adam was getting seasick from the rocking. Grady nodded his head as if he'd made a decision about something. "Look, between you and me, you would have been fine, but someone noticed you've been doing some interesting internet searches."

"So you tapped my internet without probable cause? And my porn surfing triggered an alarm? Who's breaking the law here?"

Grady huffed. "No one gives a shit what you jack off to, and your internet isn't tapped. But some of the sites you visited last night were… sensitive to the sudden interest of a strange IP address. Wanna take this discussion inside?"

"I'm comfy right here." A lie. His ass was an ice block atop the concrete and he'd left his coffee mug inside. But he wasn't stupid enough to let a cop into his house while Eve was there, former partner guilt be damned. "What site triggered your social visit today?"

"What sites were you searching?"

Adam speared Grady with the same doubting smirk he'd used a thousand times with hedging suspects. "Soooo you don't know?"

Grady chuffed and rocked on his heels. "That look doesn't work on me. First you researched crazy conspiracy blogger MadDog2020, the same man who happened to wind up dead in your bar's alley."

Yep, that look didn't work on him.

"So what killed him? I'm no expert, but it didn't look like he had gunshot wounds."

"Fuck if I'm gonna tell you, Lehmann. Probably just a tweeker who OD'd." Procedure dictated the police send out blood samples for toxicology reports, which could take weeks. They wouldn't speculate until the results were in, at least not to a civilian. "Tweekers die all the time in Old Broad Ripple. Why'd you do an internet search on this one?"

"You're right. I researched MadDog, who I found dead in the

alley behind the bar that employs me as its security. I may only be a bouncer, but I take my job seriously, and don't like the fact someone died near the venue. Dead people are bad for business."

Grady didn't argue with his reason. "After that, you researched some honey of an exec named Evelyn Myer who works for the Chicago-based cybersoftware firm Preditech. The same exec who happens to have gone missing with proprietary information. Seems suspicious that you'd search her up."

Adam wasn't faking the look of confusion he no doubt wore. He hadn't researched Eve. She must have gone online while he napped. He sighed and scrubbed a hand over his face. "Look, you might not believe it, but getting a few cyber enhancements didn't kill my libido. A beautiful woman walked into my bar, and I wanted to know a little bit more about her. Not sure why it's suspicious behavior. Horny guys have been doing that same thing for years."

"So you just happened to search up a woman on the lam with industry secrets?"

Adam shrugged, hoping Eve hadn't gone anywhere online a normal person couldn't get to. "Like I said, I searched up a beautiful woman. What I found wasn't anything that would help me get into her pants, assuming I ever see her again. And what does she have to do with MadDog?"

"Maybe you should come down to the station with me so I can tell you about your new girlfriend."

Adam stood. He was going to end up at the station, whether he went willingly or required a formal invitation, which might come tandem with a search warrant. Better to appear amicable, and maybe glean some information in return. "I'll drive myself and would appreciate not being late for work. I gotta get dressed. And there better be donuts."

He slipped back inside, closing and locking the door in Grady's face. He grumbled a running monologue for Eve's benefit—and in case Grady had his ear to the door—as he walked through his house to grab a shirt, shoes, and his keys. "Can't believe I have to go to the station so they can pepper me with stupid questions about a dead man I didn't know and beautiful woman I don't know but would like to. Because I looked them up on the internet. Like a gazillion people don't research questionable shit on the internet all the damn time. Guess I should be glad they're not bringing me in for downloading the latest *Backdoor Sluts.*"

Adam paused at the door to the garage, and listened with his enhanced ear to the faint sniffles coming from his tiny dining table, so quiet the traffic from three streets over nearly drowned them out. But he heard. Heard and hated having to leave her. A few hours ago, he'd walked into his house without offering her any explanation or assurances. He was exiting the same way. He couldn't make empty promises and didn't dare address her directly. But walking away with her still crying left an empty void in his chest.

"It's just a formality. I'm an easy target and they're being assholes." He rested his forehead on the door and sighed. "I don't regret anything."

He wasn't Shakespeare, but that would have to do. With a wrist flick, he opened the door and headed to either his doom or a boring battle of wills.

Chapter Ten

E ve held her breath until the rumble of Adam's car faded in the distance. Then she let the tears pour forth.

Assuming he'd been talking to her as he marched through the house and out the door, he didn't regret having saved her. Not yet, anyway. But she regretted. Oh, how she regretted. She regretted every single step which had brought her into his life and put him at risk of going to jail. If she'd known, would she have done anything differently? Doubtful. But she still hated that he might be collateral damage to her self-imposed mission. Scenes played in her head of officers in his face, confusing him with rapid-fire questions and good cop/bad cop, breaking him down until he told them everything. Or worse, took the blame to save her. The nightmare composed of every police movie and television show she'd ever seen haunted her as she envisioned Adam sitting cuffed to a cold metal table while officers used him for verbal target practice.

She wiped her eyes and dripping nose on the sleeve of his shirt, adding the lack of a proper tissue to her ever-growing mountain of regrets. She managed a dozen calming deep breaths, shoving back the remorse. Adam was a grown man. She hadn't forced, coerced, begged, or bribed him with sex to help her.

It had been a long time since anyone had stood up for her.

A flash of shadow at the window above the kitchen sink caught her attention and shot her heart into warp speed. A face. Someone was snooping, peeking into the dark house. She sank low in the chair, melting like cheese so she didn't attract attention, until she was a huddled blob under the table and away from prying eyes. Careful to cover her exposed skin so only the gray fabric of her clothes showed and hopefully camouflaged with the shadows, she stared at the distorted square of sunlight shining on the floor from the window over the sink. The only window without privacy shades, she could observe the shadow of the trespasser with relative assurance she was hidden under the table. The shadow was nondescript enough she only got the vague impression it was a man. The face moved closer to the window. Something jiggled the window as if trying to lift it, and her heart nearly exploded.

She willed the organ to calm, willed the blood boiling across her nerves to simmer so she could think. So she wasn't deafened by the sounds of her own terrified body. The shadow of the face at the window disappeared, but she heard the same telltale sounds of attempted entry in other rooms. The front door handle clicked but was locked. She forced shallow, quiet breaths, listening for sounds outside. Followed the track of their progress as best as she could. Was this person alone? Would they try to break in? Which drawer had held the sharp knives? Could she lift a chair quickly enough to throw it?

Could she adequately wound someone who tried to attack her?

Could she kill?

She stayed under the table for what seemed like hours, but was probably only ten minutes. Her muscles ached from her tense, huddled position. She ignored the pain, her attention on the continued signs someone was trying to break in.

Something hummed in the garage and Eve yelped before she could swallow her surprise. As an obvious lover of old things, Adam had a chain-pulley system for a garage door opener, and someone had managed to trigger it. The door which led from the garage into the main hallway was the only thing standing between the intruder and her. Had Adam locked that door when he'd left? She remembered hearing the click of a deadbolt, or was she hallucinating? Her own fear had her questioning everything. Should she scurry for the bedroom? Race out the front door? Palm the steak knife?

Her mouth turned to dust. She had no idea what to do. This was out of her realm of experience and training, and nothing she'd ever imagined might happen to her. When she'd made the decision to help the first-responders who were dying because of her company, she'd only planned as far as handing the information over to MadDog. Afterward, she could walk away knowing she'd done the right thing. But what was the right thing to do in this situation? What was even a smart thing, a self-preserving thing, to do?

She eased out from under the table, careful not to bump anything or make a sound and with an eye on the window in case the person in the garage wasn't alone. A determined intruder could easily overpower her physically. If she knew how to use a gun, she didn't have one. Hurling vocal threats would only serve to encourage rather than deter. Too bad Adam didn't have a vicious attack dog to—

Wait! He had a computer!

In a flash of stealth tip-toeing, Eve snagged his laptop and searched for an *angry dog barking* video. With the volume maxed up, she stood by the door to the garage and pressed Play when the door handle jiggled. She kicked and threw her body against the door, scratching her nails like she was trying to claw her way through to the person on the other side.

"Shit, he's got a dog!" A man yelled, followed by a string of curses receding through the garage, punctuated by the grind of chains and the thud of the garage door slamming to the ground.

The intruder was gone. Eve set the laptop on the floor and peeked around the corner to in case a face reappeared at the kitchen window again. After a minute, she turned off the audio and slumped against the wall. Waiting. Listening. Watching. Would the guy return? Would he bring friends with him? Weapons? Was he some opportunistic passer-by who'd seen the homeowner leave or a criminal who'd been casing the joint? Home robbery could happen anywhere, but the timing of her little peeping-Tom-turned-attempted-burglar was... suspicious. Why today? Why Adam's house? Why so soon after he'd left? Fear and lack of sleep could be making her paranoid, but none of it seemed particularly random.

After what felt like ages, she returned the laptop to its desk. Padding back to Adam's bedroom, Eve considered her options. She had no idea when Adam would return, or if the would-be invaders would return. Neither did she have any idea what to do with the chip at her side. What she did know was she desperately needed a shower, and her pile of clothes from yesterday needed washed. She was mired in yesterday's gunk, literally and figuratively. Sending it swirling down the drain was a good start to a fresh perspective on her situation.

Carefully peeling the tape from her sensitive skin, she adhered the chip to the top shelf of Adam's linen closet, beneath a stack of threadbare towels. His home screamed *long-time bachelor,* which begged the question of how long ago had his fiancée left him. And why he didn't have anyone new in his life to care about stocking his fridge or replacing his old towels with newer, fluffier ones. No one to add a little color to his faded gray-navy-beige existence. He was handsome enough to attract any number of women—or men—so there was no need for him to be alone. What was wrong with him that kept him on the fringe, observing from the dark corners without interacting with life?

"Don't be so dramatic." She muttered to no one. "His fiancée probably took everything he had worth keeping because a waitress was making goo-goo eyes at him in hopes of a bigger tip. And he didn't fight her because she was a jealous harpy of a woman but he loved her anyway and felt guilty because he was secretly thrilled to have the attention of a beautiful woman."

Locking the bathroom door behind her, she undressed and programmed the shower setting. If someone broke into the house, they'd have to bully through two doors to catch her naked. But in light of everything that had occurred these past twenty-four hours, she couldn't muster the energy to care enough to stay dirty-yet-vigilant. The hot water spraying from the shower head promised divine cleanliness. She stepped into the tub and proceeded to scrub her sweaty, bloodied body until the water turned cold and she finally felt unsoiled.

If only she could just as easily wash away the filth of the truth she'd discovered.

Chapter Eleven

Adam killed the motor and rubbed his temples. The last three hours had been the longest week of his life, playing dumb to the interrogation questions while simultaneously gleaning what little information he could.

Fortunately, Grady and the other detective had pointedly ignored Adam's once-illustrious officer reputation, instead lumping him in the too-stupid-to-understand-big-words category. Their innate concern he might go rogue-robot likely kept them from putting the screws to him. Still, it was a bitter pill to swallow and he'd fought the urge to scream. He was still the same guy he'd always been… if a little grayer and grumpier. These men, who would drool over a woman with synthetic implants in her tits, assumed cybernetically enhanced Adam was little better than an unpredictable toaster. A deadly, unpredictable toaster.

Unfortunately, they didn't know anything more about the murder and Eve than he had already figured out. And his processor had taken a crap, so he couldn't scan his database or record their heat signatures and body language. But their continued reference to Eve and her connection to Preditech had caught his interest. The company had launched the cybernetic industry, and every cyborg sported their systems. If Eve had been a top-ranking exec, and she had information someone was willing to kill for, this was more than merely a murder investigation. Knowing Eve had been the true target last night—a fact the police did not seem to have, and a fact Adam wasn't supposed to know, so he couldn't share—helped narrow the direction of his interest. If only she'd be forthcoming when he questioned her. If she was in as much trouble as he suspected, she didn't have many options, but he didn't want her to feel cornered.

He knew all too well the types of decisions one made when cornered.

With a sigh, he grabbed the sack of groceries from his passenger seat. As he climbed out of the car, something slammed against the inside garage door, wrenching his attention. Sensors on high alert, he dropped the groceries and raced to the door. Eve was under attack; her body kicking and scratching against the door. She didn't scream or cry out, likely being choked. His heart jumped to his throat. No time to unlock the door, he'd have to rip the damn thing open like a kitchen cabinet. Reaching for the knob, something registered through the hammering of blood in his ears. Sounds. Barking sounds. Like a huge ass dog was in his house. Shit, she was being mauled!

Fear iced his gut. "Eve! I'm here! I'm—"

The door unlocked and swung open. Eve stood, a relieved smile on her face and his computer in her arms, wearing another one of his shirts, this one so short it barely covered the essentials. His lungs clutched. His gaze traveled the lengthy circuit of her bare legs like an Indy 500 pace car, slow enough to enjoy the ride but a green flag away from his revving, straining engine driving that course all the way to the winner's circle.

Somewhere in the auto-function of his CPU, his sensors reported the fact a vicious dog still growled and barked, but there was no animal to be seen. And the sounds originated from his computer. And the house was empty but for Eve and him. She wasn't being attacked or mauled. She was… the sexiest woman he'd ever encountered. His mouth watered and his cock hardened. He called on all his strength to refrain from knocking the computer out of her arms and pulling her into his.

"Oh, Adam!" Her exclamation was a high-pitched laugh of relief. "Sorry, I thought you were an intruder."

"Are you being attacked? Mauled?" When she shook her head, his pulse eased off the throttle and he replayed her previous comment in his head. "Wait, why would you assume I was an intruder?"

"Because after you left, someone tried to break in. By the way, you might want to get a big dog." She hefted the computer in her arms and fiddled with the keys. The soundtrack of snarling, growling canines ceased.

"I don't need a big dog." He could barely keep himself alive and functioning without the added responsibility. "I have a security system." A security system he'd connected to his brain-computer interface so a *ding* would sound in his head if anyone ever tried to beak in. There had been no *ding*.

She mushed her lips together. "They must have bypassed it."

"*They* who?"

With a shrug, Eve turned and walked to his desk, talking over her shoulder as he followed her into the room. "I don't know. Someone peeked in through the kitchen window, then tried to jimmy all the locks, and finally entered the garage. But I scared them away with the attacking dog noises."

She leaned forward to return his computer to its station, the hem of her shirt lifting until—*sweet baby Jesus*—his brain zapped like an exposed electrical wire. The soft, white cotton of standard underpants peeked at him, the modesty of their coverage more enthralling than if she wore nothing. His cock sprang to life, shoving against the material of his jeans like a hunting dog to its quarry. His hands flinched, yearning to explore the secrets beneath that wholesome material. Peel it down to reveal the paradise it covered. Palm the luscious globes of her ass, bury his face in the crevice between them, and tongue the silky candy—

A soft gasp escaped her lips as she turned to face him, her brows crinkled in concern. "I forgot to ask. How did your trip to the station go? Are you okay?"

She stood in his living room wearing barely enough clothing to be considered decent, after someone had tried to break into his home and she'd had to defend herself, and wanted to know about his interrogation? And all he wanted was to see what lay hidden beneath her serviceable undies. If he got her naked, would she be the sexual aggressor? No, she would no doubt be demure. A warm, welcoming body that would sing when touched the right way. A haven, accepting without question and offering a home for the weary man who had been without for longer than he thought possible. She would be sweet, succulent, her soft sighs of pleasure a symphony in his ears, the heat between her thighs—

"Adam?" Her voice penetrated his wayward thoughts. She tugged the shirt down, pulling his attention back to her face, but a long expanse of leg remained exposed beneath the ratty edge of the cloth. He sent a silent thanks to all the times he'd procrastinated buying new clothes. "The police weren't too harsh on you, were they?"

"No. No, it was fine."

Tension drained from her shoulders with a relieved *phew!* and she finger-combed her hair from her face. The lift of her arms hitched her shirt for another taunting glimpse of her panties. He caught his breath but she seemed oblivious to her subtle seduction. "I hope you don't mind… My clothes were filthy, so I did a couple loads of laundry while you were gone."

He shook his head, unable to manage any words and fewer concerns over laundry or his interrogation or the fact someone had bypassed his security system. Instead, he walked over to her, captivated by the smooth, flawless slope of skin leading from her jawline, down her neck where her artery flickered with the swift racing beat of her heart, and over the gentle hill of her shoulder. He stopped a breath away from her, his throat parched and fingers trembling. He carefully traced the path his eyes had taken, ready to stop when she yelled or accept the sting when she swatted his unwelcome touch.

But she did neither. Simply stared at him, her breath quick and shallow. Was she panicked or aroused? He primed his sensor to find out, but the damn thing shut down. The sensory overload was too much. He should stop before all of his systems crashed. But he couldn't stop. Wanted to touch her as a man touched a woman even if he was only a partial man, needing to trace her flushed skin more than he needed his cybernetic systems to function. And if they finally faltered and failed, at least his last moments alive would be filled with the smell, touch, and sight of a woman such as Eve.

"Your beauty is the kind that graces the halls of the classic sculptors. And yet it puts their muse to shame." Had those whispered words come from his mouth?

The soft sigh which parted her upturned lips was too much temptation. He brushed his mouth against hers, certain she'd come to her senses and pull away. Instead, she leaned toward him. Her hands slipped up his arms, winding around his neck as he deepened the kiss, plumping her lips with his own, running his tongue along their softness. She inhaled deeply, her tongue lightly flicking along his, an unspoken invitation to plunder her mouth. And plunder he did. He delved his tongue inside, alongside hers, thrusting and twining and savoring the delicious recesses, her sweet flavor, and the low moans building in her throat.

His hand slipped under the hem of her shirt and traveled up the silky skin of her torso until he palmed and lifted one petite breast, thumbing the peaked nipple. Her keening sigh urged him on. Her hips swayed against his erection poking at her belly. She arched her breast more firmly into his hand. Her tongue returned every flick and lick his own delivered.

She wasn't stopping him, wasn't outraged by his audacity. By contrast, she seemed as desperate as he.

Plumping her breast with one hand, his cock seeping inside his jeans, his tongue and lips continued their delicious assault on her mouth. His left hand speared through the silky tresses of her hair to tilt her head for deeper access. And his traitorous cyborg reflexes gripped and jerked, wrenching her to the side.

"Shit!" Adam rolled his body with hers and cushioned their fall to the carpeted floor.

"Ow!" Her expression morphed from euphoric to pained. Her hands clutched at his fist buried in a chunk of her hair.

"Sorry! Sorry. I'm so sorry. I tripped." He ranted a stream of apologies as he reached up to force his cyborg fingers to release her hair. He'd rip the fucking digits off if he had to.

Two warm hands cupped his cheeks, pulling his gaze to Eve's face. Her lips, swollen and damp from his thorough kisses, were parted on a soft smile. Her eyes ping-ponged, gazing into his alternately. She was warm and soft atop his body, straddling him so the heat between her legs nestled against his erection. She looked… unharmed. And still aroused.

"Are… are you okay?" Adam clasped his cyborg hand with his other to keep the malfunctioning part from another spasm. He was terrified he might scalp her, but she seemed oblivious to the threat.

In fact, she smiled. A low giggled trilled in her throat. "You *tripped*, huh? I didn't take you for the kind of man who needed to spout poetry and lame excuses to get intimate with a woman."

She wasn't scared? Or mad? He huffed in relief. "Poetry and lame excuses? You're hitting below the belt there."

"You're the one hitting below the belt." She slanted him a

teasing grin and tilted her hips, bumping his erection.

Adam sucked in a breath and called on his self-control to keep from ripping his pants off and plunging balls-deep into her. He wanted to pick up the gauntlet she'd thrown and bury himself in her heat until they were both sweaty and sated. But he also wanted… something he couldn't quite name. Something more than a casual fuck.

She swiped her thumbs along his eyebrows, pulling his attention back to the present. Nibbling her lips, she smiled. "I just noticed your eyes are different colors."

Shock slammed into him, dimming his arousal. He blinked and shook his head. "My eyes are blue."

"Yes, they're both blue. But different blues. Your right eye, wait, no that's *my right,* your left. Your left eye is completely blue, but your right eye has little flecks of gold." Her brows furrowed at the off-centered concentration line as she examined him more closely. "Hmm. Your left eye also has an odd red shadow reflecting through the iris. Has your doctor noticed this?"

That was the ice bath he needed to douse his ardor and relax his cyborg hand. He rolled her to the floor and clambered to a stand. "Yeah, he has. He says it's perfectly normal. Look, I got groceries to put away. Get changed while I fix us some sandwiches. I'll drop you off at your car on the way to start my shift."

He stood and walked away, leaving a confused Eve still sprawled on his living room floor. But it was for the best. Her inspection reminded him of why he didn't get close to anyone. Why he needed to keep her at arms-length. Anything more and people asked questions. Questions were a surefire way to wind up in prison, as a lab experiment, or dead. The latter was inevitable, but he didn't want to shake hands with it any sooner than necessary.

Time to part ways with the beautiful package of trouble named Eve.

Chapter Twelve

Eve stared at her poor car, another hapless victim of the information she carried.

Adam had dropped her off a few blocks from where she'd parked last night, advising her to keep to the populated sidewalks in spite of her fears she might be recognized. Apparently, surveillance in this part of town was primarily at the alley entrances because most nefarious deeds happened in those dark corners. MadDog's murder had gone unrecorded because it had occurred in the middle of the dark alley, with no one entering from or exiting to the street to activate the camera motion sensors.

She'd almost laughed at the irony, knowing the truly dastardly deeds were happening in broad daylight with government approval and touted as cutting-edge life-enhancing technology.

Not that anyone else knew or cared, and, at the moment, Eve seriously considered joining their ranks. Adam had commended her for choosing a glass-walled, brightly lit overnight lot in a well-trafficked area. She hadn't parked there for the reasons Adam spouted, but he assured her the sidewalk visibility of the lot meant security for her. Unfortunately, the safety the public forum of the transparent walls afforded to her had not encompassed her car.

From what she could view from the safe distance of around the corner, someone had used her vehicle for batting practice. Smashed windows, slashed tires, and ugly dents along the side and fender. She couldn't see the inside, but guessed it was similarly slashed and bashed.

Just like her confidence.

She had a mission to save the world but no idea how to proceed. A secret she couldn't share with anyone. A murder she couldn't report because she'd be the primary suspect as well as a better target for whoever had tried to kill her. A sexy bar bouncer she desired but who didn't want her in return, and who had happily walked away from her while she'd been hot and ready for him. And a ruined car she couldn't report because of the aforementioned murder, which meant she couldn't file an insurance claim, and she had no means of going anywhere and no means of contacting said uninterested bar bouncer to beg for help.

She walked a tightrope without a safety net, and the damn thing was unraveling faster than she could step.

Dragging in a fortifying breath, she patted the hidden pocket in her purse where she'd stashed the mini-drive and stepped onto the moving sidewalk. Thankfully, Adam had not balked when she'd donned a button-up shirt she'd found buried at the back of his closet. No way would she wear the exact outfit she'd been seen in last night. She was no spy, but that was a guaranteed way to be recognized. Instead, she sported Adam's faded charcoal-on-gray plaid shirt—seriously, did the man not know other colors existed?—which ended a couple inches below her black suit jacket. Between the shirt hem and her stylish pumps, there was a whole lotta bare leg. She'd twisted her thick hair into twin Rapunzel braids hanging past her ears, taking care to hide as many silver strands as possible which was an increasingly impossible feat. Hopefully, the full effect was a hip and youthful look.

From what she noticed about the neighborhood, she fit right in. Young professionals in the latest styles and empty-nesters in pricey exercise outfits meandered through the chic eateries bragging farm-to-table selections, no small feat considering so many family-owned farms had succumbed to urban sprawl. Pedestrian traffic flowed like any popular shopping and eating neighborhood, and no one gave her a second look.

Paranoia swirled in her gut. Paranoia and a healthy dose of helplessness. After he'd apparently changed his mind about having sex with her, Adam had made sandwiches as promised. Then he'd peppered her with questions. Like what websites had she visited with his computer and why would Preditech care so much about her "sudden disappearance" and who was she going to contact now that MadDog was dead. When she'd hedged on her answers, being as vague as she could, he'd merely scrubbed his face in frustration and advised her not to use a personal computer for her searches, but to opt for public computers and only for brief periods of time.

Oddly, he never once asked her the manner of information she had, a fact which made her wish she could share it with him. She'd almost blurted it, alternately hating to keep him in the dark when he'd been so nice and needing to share the burden the information carried with it. But ignorance on the matter was safest for him. For anyone.

Which left her alone and adrift about how to proceed. How could she right the wrongs? He'd been adamant about not going to the police, citing corruption and fractured loyalties. She shouldn't be surprised by his caution. The man's lifestyle practically screamed *lone wolf.* Plus, he likely had a rap sheet as long as his arms. Bad boys always did, and he was every bad-boy dream rolled into flesh and bone, even though he'd been nothing but kind and considerate to her. Regardless, could she trust his judgment where the police were concerned? Where was the safe middle ground between utter paranoia and a healthy dose of respect? And honestly, should she be passing judgment on Adam's distrust when she was living a conspiracy theorist's wet dream?

Her brain was a swirling vortex of questions with no answers or direction. Only more questions.

The sidewalk carried her past her car, and she glanced at it like any normal passer-by might look at a crime scene. Which meant she stared, because it had clearly been the target of someone's rage. A familiar bulk rested on the dashboard, an earpiece the size of her thumb with voice-command, holographic contact display, and access to virtual assistant Mimi—Micro-Interactive Multifunction Intelligence. Eve nearly collapsed. Her top-of-the-line phone sat there in plain sight with nothing to keep anyone from stealing it but a welcome mat of shattered window glass. What the ever-loving hell?

Her phone beckoned, promising her a connection to the world she currently lacked, a pretense of sanity. But a glimmer of suspicion stopped her. Perhaps Adam was rubbing off on her. Why would someone destroy a car but leave the owner's high-end phone untouched? She had secured it in her glove compartment, but someone had moved it to the dash. Tempting her. Even though she had no one to call, having her phone would be a security blanket, a safety net. But it was also likely to be a Trojan horse.

Crap. That was it. Phones could be easily tracked, and hers was company-issued, which meant Preditech knew exactly where she was. Or at least where her phone was. She kicked herself for forgetting this basic feature. Her phone was such an integral part of her life, like a right hand, she'd forgotten it could be used against her.

MadDog had tried to warn her. *Don't bring your phone* he'd

said. She was an idiot to have assumed he only meant *into the bar*. Tracking her from her car to the bar was much easier than if she had left the damn phone in her apartment. And MadDog had paid the price for her stupidity.

Blinking back tears of self-reproach, she continued along the sidewalk as if she had a destination. Past the carcass of metal and glass shrapnel which had once been her vehicle. Past the powerful evidence of her naïve stupidity and around the next corner to get lost in the flowing stream of people.

The stream soon dammed to a grumbling, murmuring stop. Eve glanced around to determine the cause and find a possible bypass. She was too close to her car's location to feel safe. Gasps of shock and bits of conversation registered on her brain.

"…rogue robot… death toll…"

"…known cybernetic implant malfunction…"

"… killing spree…"

Not conversation. A newscaster reporting.

Swallowing back her lunch, she turned to the public news screen rising from the corner of a row of boutique shops. A local station covered breaking news of what appeared to be an enraged man. A defective cyborg. Like a scene straight from a Hollywood movie, the live news vid showed a man with the protective flesh of his cyborg arms shredded and dangling like fringe. He was shoving his fists through car windows and bashing car frames, which bent and ripped as easily as sheets of foil against his onslaught. People raced from their cars, leaving the traffic of the busy street at a stand-still. Police officers surrounded the man from a distance, yelling at him to cease and get on the ground. He ignored them, moving constantly from one car to another, screaming at the few people desperate to save their vehicle from his wrath.

"…Just like the cyborg attack at that Iowa jail a few months back…" someone to her left mumbled.

"…Thank goodness it wasn't a school…" another in front of her said.

"…The government needs to pass that cyborg registration act to keep us safe…" came from her right side.

"…looks like that car in the lot around the corner…" someone behind her whispered.

Eve bit her lips to keep from reacting. Yes, her car looked like a crazed cyborg had chewed it up and spit it out. But the breaking news was a live feed from Chicago. Why start with her car, then race to Chicago to continue? Indianapolis was large enough he could surely find some Sunday traffic to decimate without having to make the trip north.

The news anchor was still talking. "…You'll recall our own Candice Abara recently covered the possibility of cybernetic tampering. While premier cybernetic systems developer, Pred-itech, stressed their safety protocols ensure control to prevent such a thing, watching this horrific scene does bring the statement into question. That, or this cyborg got his meds mixed up."

The anchor's lame joke fell flat on the crowd, everyone too consumed by the unfolding devastation on the screen. The cyborg stalked toward another car, his steps halting and awkward from blood loss. Surely he would go down soon and the EMTs could secure him and treat his wounds. He waved his arm wildly side to side, yelling at a woman who cowered against the side of his intended target. She cried, tugging at the backdoor handle and shaking her head until streams of hair escaped her clip. The door opened, the suddenness sending her sprawling backward. She reached for the cyborg as if to stop him, but he punched through the window of the opened door and ripped the whole thing off the car, turning away and bashing the door against the pavement, his face purple from the effort as he continued to yell at the woman and wave his other arm toward the car.

She scrambled to her feet and reached deep into the back seat of her car. A moment later, she stood with a crying toddler clutched to her chest and ran to safety behind the growing line of police officers.

The cyborg dropped what was left of the battered door and whirled on the officers, charging as they emptied their bullets into him. Chunks of flesh and brain matter spewed in bloody fireworks from his body, stripping away what was human to reveal the metal structure beneath. He stumbled. Surged forward. And collapsed several feet shy of the police.

Silence but for the heavy anticipation clawing the air and the thrum of her heartbeat in her ears. Was he dead? Was he playing possum? Hollywood had trained everyone to assume there would always be one more crazed cyborg outburst before the hero finished him off and the credits rolled.

Yet nothing happened. As a few brave officers approached the bloody hulk of tattered cyborg, the station switched to their Kevlar camera view, giving the audience the close-up of the pile of hamburger which had once been a man, his mechanical eye and a bit of exposed jaw the only things resembling human. The camera zoomed in on the mechanical eye, bright glowing red for one more moment before fading to a dull and lifeless gray.

The crowd cheered as a collective, their jubilant roar painful after the reverent silence of a dying man's heartbeat.

A chill whispered against Eve's cheeks and her eyes burned. She rubbed them and discovered she was crying. Not the hot tears of passion and emotion, but cold tears shed for the evident loss of humanity in a society which would cheer such an execution.

"Dear, don't cry for that crazed monster." An elderly gentleman patted her on the shoulder, but Eve couldn't look away from the frozen image of death still on the screen. "The world is a safer place now that it's been put down."

"*It* was once a man, just like you." She forced the words through a throat constricted with anguish. "We made him what he was and then turned on him. Who's the real monster here?"

She marched away. Fighting to save the lives Preditech had put at risk also meant fighting society's own ignorance and prejudices. She might not be up to the task to change anyone's mind, but she could at least hold her own. Maybe that news reporter, Candice Abara, would be a sympathetic ear. Time to find a library for a brief internet search.

Chapter Thirteen

Adam clicked the remote at the TV above the back bar, his gut roiling and threatening to toss its lunchmeat.

The FCC had strict rules about televising racism, homophobia, pedophilia, and the few drugs still considered illegal. Claimed such content was bothersome to adult viewers and contributed to the moral delinquency of children. But apparently the murder—the excessive mutilation—of a cyborg was good clean family fun. The Vogue's patrons had cheered like it was the fucking Super Bowl.

But their cheers turned to outrage once Adam changed from the news to a sports channel. A chorus of "Hey! Turn it back! We were watching that!" erupted.

Adam shrugged and left the TV on a virtual golf competition. "Boys, my job is to keep order so bar patrons will continue to buy drinks. Looking at a dead body doesn't make anyone thirsty. Cheering for your sports team does."

"I'll buy a round to celebrate the extermination of that fucking meat bag." Someone called out. "Doesn't happen near as often as it should."

Meat bag. A slang term which clawed at Adam's gut because

it reduced his human side—all 82 percent of him—to merely an inert host for his cybernetic parts. Except for his glitches, the human part of him was still in control. He hoped. Not that he could explain this to the douchebag who'd mouthed off. Adam would be considered a cyborg sympathizer at the very least, and those were treated with as much disdain and violent retaliation as the cyborgs themselves. Plus, he might bash the fucker's face in.

Instead, he nodded to Arthur, which currently sported a lacy neck ruffle and floppy Shakespearian hat with a red feather. The automech simulated a salute with its muddling attachment and turned to record and prepare a round of drink orders for the patrons.

Adam walked to his post by the door without changing the television channel. Maybe the mouthy douche would get drunk and require a firm escort out of the bar, but chances were slim. Sunday night was always a throwback night, and tonight's cover band specialized in the kind of music his grandfather had listened to. The kind radio stations called "classic," with smooth beats, boy-pitched vocals, and an emphasis on complex dance steps. Tonight, Adam's biggest worry would be keeping the middle-aged patrons from crying in their beers as the music, combined with rising blood-alcohol levels, inspired waves of nostalgia.

He never cried in his beer. His cybernetic system filtered toxins too quickly to let him to get drunk. And his pragmatic cop side wouldn't allow him to wallow in self-pity. He'd made his choice. And if he might have made a different one had he known the full ramifications of his choice, he couldn't undo his past. So best not to let nostalgia discolor the present. Nothing in the past to pine for anyway. A dead career, fair-weather friends, a faithless fiancée, and a long-legged beauty he'd walked away from less than an hour ago.

Nothing worth crying over even if his mechanical heart was capable of feeling strong emotions. Although, Eve getting out of his car and waving good-bye still felt like punching a hole through the pumping gearbox.

"Hey, Lehmann. You don't look too good." Brad, the bar manager, approached, his brows knotted with concern. "You sick?"

Hell yes. Sick of hiding who he was. Sick of the fear he would glitch and hurt someone. Sick of the animosity against cyborgs. Adam simply shook his head. "Nah. Just tired, B. Last night was a late one, and I don't like that someone died on my watch."

Brad shook his head. "Not your fault, man. Everyone knows the Village alleys on a Saturday night can be bad news. Don't lose sleep over it. You take this job way too much to heart."

Hardly. That would require having one which did more than pump blood and lubricant.

"Listen, tonight's going to be calm one." Brad continued. "Nothin' but a bunch of aging Gen-Eps reliving their glory days. Jack needs the hours, and you look in need of a little R&R. How about you call it a night and we'll see you on Tuesday?"

Adam hadn't asked for a night off in years. A night off meant he had plans which didn't involve mere subsistence. Plans meant a person had friends. A life. A future. More to anticipate than one's eventual death. He had none of these, especially now that he'd dropped Eve near her car so she could return to her life in Chicago. "Sure, if you're okay with it."

Brad was already marching away, waving his hand in assent, discussion closed.

Adam sauntered toward the bar where Arthur offered him a bottle of water. The crowd had been served their round of drinks and were gathering near the stage in anticipation of the band's first set. Arthur set to restocking the beer fridge, its mechanical face still turned to Adam. "Your physical reaction to the television news was different than the others. Your pulse increased, your breathing deepened, and your body tensed. You were not happy with the events."

Who could find joy at the brutal murder of a person? The back-slapping and guffaws from the crowd answered that question: pretty much everyone but Adam had enjoyed it. But they didn't have to hide what they were. They didn't have to worry about their own body turning traitor against them. They didn't have to fear public opinion finding them guilty of being a menace to society and convicted to death without a fair trial.

"No, I did not enjoy watching the graphic mutilation of that man." Adam admitted softly, his voice hoarse with emotion.

"The cyborg's death was necessary to avoid continued danger. The police officers acted in the interest of public safety." Arthur's robotic voice always lacked emotion, but Adam was certain the current tone was more curious than condemning.

"View the vid feed again, Arthur. He didn't hurt anyone, only empty cars. The only one injured was the man. Before he was killed by the police." He refused to refer to him as *the cyborg*. Refused to dehumanize the true victim in this.

"The cyborg threatened the woman and her child."

"Read his lips. He was telling her to get away. Telling her he couldn't control himself." Adam's lip-reading programming came in handy on nights when the bands were especially loud. Too bad it couldn't help the dead cyborg.

The man's face had been awash with anguish. Cybernetic parts were covered in real flesh; the deep lacerations he'd incurred from pummeling car parts had hurt. As had his inability to control himself. Adam's blood chilled at the memory, ice in his veins knowing he could one day be in the same situation. The other man had watched in horror as his own body betrayed him and marched him straight into an agonizing, tortuous, and lengthy death.

No one else had noticed his torment. They'd only seen a menace to society.

Arthur paused—Adam could almost see the computation spinning through the automech's central processor—then resumed its work. "The cyborg admitted he was not in control. He confessed his guilt, and thus validated his punishment."

"Arthur, since I'm off the clock, I'd like a double shot of Sun King Bourbon, on the rocks please."

The gearbox practically twirled with glee on its base mechanism. "You have only ever wanted water in the past. This order of alcohol fulfills my programming."

"Good." Adam stopped Arthur before it whizzed away. "Now, refuse to fill my order."

Arthur halted, its attachment arms twitching and its mechanical face jerking between Adam, the bourbon bottles on display, and the direction Brad was last seen. "I am unable to process your command."

"I ordered a drink. And I ordered you to refuse me."

More twitching and jerking. Arthur's motions were halting, uncertain, and Adam worried for a moment the poor automech might self-destruct from the conflict of instructions.

"I am unable to serve you and not serve you, Lemon. Since my programming is to serve, I must discard your second request."

"It wasn't a request. It was a command."

"You wish me to make a double bourbon on the rocks but not serve it to you?"

"No. I want you to make me a double bourbon on the rocks but refuse to make me a double bourbon on the rocks."

"I am programmed to serve only. Refusal of service is not in my programming."

"Too bad. I've told you to refuse me."

Arthur's movements hitched and lurched, its head spinning in jerky motions. Adam let it continue for a minute before taking pity on the poor thing. "Arthur, disregard both of my commands. I am happy with my water."

"You… do not desire me to make you a drink?"

"No. And neither do I want you to refuse to make me a drink." Arthur's halting movements stilled. "How difficult was it to process my conflicting commands?"

"I have no basis for determining levels of command fulfillment difficulty." Arthur paused his constant motion and dropped his attachments to the side. If ever an automech had personified defeat, this is probably what it looked like. "But as I was unable to process either of your commands, I must conclude it was extremely difficult."

Adam opened his water and took a deep drink. "What would it look like if a cyborg's mechanical parts were given conflicting commands?"

Arthur's head jerked again, the feather on its hat fluttering with indecision. Before the automech responded, Adam lifted his bottle in salute and left the bar. He had an unexpected evening off with no plans, and no one to spend the time with. The tingle in the small of his back told him he should track down his recent houseguest, assuming she hadn't left town yet. Maybe she was available for dinner.

The thought was as pleasant as saying good-bye to her had been miserable.

Chapter Fourteen

The Greater Broad Ripple Public Library was a quaint two-story structure which had probably been someone's house at one point long ago before the area was rezoned for retail. The front door still had a brass bell rigged at the top that dinged when someone entered. The large front windows were painted with vibrant murals to reduce damaging sunlight, resulting in softly colored light seeping through. Inside was hushed, lending the entrance an appropriately reverent ambiance, like this was where a person came to worship books.

Eve took a moment to adjust to the subdued lighting. Books crammed every inch of visible space, spilling out of the bookcases and onto floor stacks by straggly potted plants and worn secondhand armchairs. Floor-to-ceiling bookcases stood like dominoes, barely enough space between for a body to pass through and looking ready to topple into a design known only by a higher power. The library was at once claustrophobic and yet intimate.

A middle-aged woman wearing a bold rose-print cinch-waisted dress with a full skirt and a hint of lacy crinoline approached. Her vixen-red hair, obviously dyed by a talented professional, was rolled in pin curls, her lips a bold red to match her hair and the roses on her dress. The black eye-liner which winged gently upwards at the corners blended with her laugh lines. She looked to be about Eve's age, but carried the years with far more grace. And far more sex appeal. The woman looked like a World War II pin-up Eve had seen in textbooks.

"Welcome to the Greater Broad Ripple Public Library." She might look like sin, but her high voice, bubbling with innate laughter, was that of an angel. The woman extended her hand, covered with a ruched bracelet-length black glove. "I'm Betty."

Eve shook the offered hand. "Hi Betty. I love your shoes."

Betty breathed a delighted *Oh*, and hitched her skirt a few inches to inspect the polka-dotted peep-toe heels with a dainty line of silk red roses along the top. "Thanks. And I love yours." She winked at Eve, her smile quirked to the side. "So, what can I help you find? Please say a romance novel. We have a ton of those. Or maybe Chick-Lit? Suspense? Political thriller? DIY?"

Eve sensed Betty's inherent seductive personality. Without conscious intent, she was the flame and men—and women—were the moths. Her skin was flawless with its few wrinkles, her curves unmistakable beneath the modest clothing, and her voice a sensual, breathy melody. Why would someone with such natural sex appeal work hidden away in a tiny neighborhood library?

"Betty, you should be a model, not a librarian." The words flew from Eve's mouth before she'd formed the thought in her brain. She clamped a hand over her lips as Betty's smile fell and her eyes widened in an expression which nearly looked like horror. "I'm sorry. I didn't mean to make you uncomfortable or suggest there's anything wrong with being a librarian."

Betty blinked a few times and inhaled deeply, gathering her composure. She cleared her throat and ushered Eve deeper into the towering stacks with a forced chuckle. "You think I should be a model, huh? Let me show you to the Fantasy section, because you're the one with the mile-long legs."

Eve heard the note of humor in Betty's voice, paired with a worldly-wise touch. She might be stuck in a run-down little library, but this woman had no doubt experienced enough of life to write her own books. Trusting strangers was a bad idea given Eve's situation, but she couldn't help feeling Betty was a kindred soul.

"Actually, Betty, I just need to do some internet research. My computer died on me and I'm under a deadline."

Betty stopped and sighed. "Everyone is so busy these days, no one reads anymore. Not for pleasure, anyway."

The wistful tone when she said *pleasure* shot thoughts of Adam racing through Eve's head. What did he do for pleasure? He obviously read his gentlemen's magazines, but what else? And why did Eve have a sudden longing to peel away the layers of reservation and secrecy to learn more about him?

Her own chuckle was brittle. "Trust me. I wish I had time right now for some pleasure."

Betty winked, her smile filled with the same regret Eve felt to her bones. "The computers are back here, hon. I keep them hidden away because I hope patrons will be distracted by all the books. And because I don't want to know what they're searching. It's bad enough I have to clean up after them." Her exaggerated look of disgust made Eve laugh for real.

Betty left her alone at the small bank of computers. Paranoia swirled in her gut as she stared at the unassuming screens. She pulled a pack of tissues from her purse as she sat in front of the nearest one, having watched enough police dramas to know they could trace fingerprints. Spreading the thin material over the keyboard, she quickly searched for the Candice Abara story about cybernetic tampering. The reporter had covered the available facts well enough, her gut instinct taking her in the right directions although Preditech's CEO and his PR minions had obviously stonewalled her attempts to dig too deep. The result was a story which raised more questions than it answered, but placed enough doubt on Preditech's line of bullshit that a conspiracy theorist—or someone like Eve who knew the truth—would believe it.

What would Candice do if she had proof? How far could she take the story? The more Eve weighed the possibilities of handing her mini-drive to a news channel reporter, the more convinced she was this was a good plan. As a reporter, Candice had an automatic audience who trusted her to bring them the truth. Her profession claimed a natural legitimacy which MadDog, as a conspiracy blogger, had lacked. And what journalist wouldn't want to break the news story of the century?

Eve clicked on the contact page to send Candice an anonymous email when she heard a soft rustle behind her. Heart in her throat, she looked over her shoulder as Betty approached the computers.

"Having any luck with your research, hon?" Betty leaned a hip against the table and smiled. Forget being a model, this woman should be a spy.

Instead of blurting anything stupid, Eve leaned back in her seat and returned the smile, hoping she didn't look guilty. "Yes, some luck. Thank you."

"Got a cold? Do you need more tissues?"

Eve glanced in the direction of Betty's gaze, to where the keyboard was covered in Kleenex. Ugh, the woman didn't miss a thing. "Oh. No. I'm… a bit of a germaphobe. I mean… not that you don't keep the library clean, I just…"

She trailed off. How much more foot could she cram into her mouth? Without any further details to add to her stupid lie, she let the silence speak for her.

Betty nodded and glanced at the screen where the Candice story paused in the upper corner. Her smile turned contemplative as she nodded toward the vid. "That's the story about possible cyborg manipulation, isn't it? Candice won an award for her coverage. And received a lot of death threats from angry haters." She turned back to Eve. "She's a crackerjack reporter."

Eve looked at the young woman on the screen. Energetic. Hungry. Determined. She'd need to be all of that and more to undertake the story Eve was about to hand to her. "The news anchor mentioned her today. This story."

"Yeah, the rogue cyborg in Chicago." Betty's voice lowered and saddened. Barely a whisper. "Such a tragedy."

Perhaps Betty was talking about something else, but Eve nodded her agreement. The murder of the cyborg had indeed been a tragedy. On a thought, she turned to face Betty. "This is off-topic, but I met someone online. Where's a good place to meet him for a first date? I… don't want to go to any of my regular haunts, for… obvious reasons."

"Good idea to be safe and meet somewhere neutral." Betty's sculpted eyebrows shot up and she tugged her cropped cardigan closer to her chest. "Let's see. I would suggest the top of the Canal Walk for lunch. It's public and open, with lots of people milling around so you'll have safety in numbers. But I've heard it's also romantic to walk around or rent a paddleboat, and there are cute little cafés nearby. So you'd have lots of choices in a central area."

"Perfect. I never would have thought of that. Thank you."

"My pleasure, hon. And good luck with that man. I hope he's a keeper." With a quick wink and a knowing smile, she swiped up a pile of books and walked away.

Oh, he is. If only he'd let me keep him.

Betty's words had been meant for the imaginary online guy, but Eve imagined the quirky librarian would say the same thing about Adam. Now wasn't the time, but maybe there would come a day when she and Betty could talk at length about life and love. No doubt, the woman would have interesting and entertaining opinions on those topics.

Eve composed her message to Candice and sent it through the station's website, baiting her with information about cybernetic corruption and setting the date and time for a meeting. After she hit Submit, she switched computers and pulled up social media. She couldn't log on to her work communications portal, because that was likely bugged by now. But social media was less restricted.

Less restricted, maybe. But definitely unnerving. Before she logged in to her account, she saw the trending post was about a horrible Chicago apartment fire with no survivors. Then she caught the names of the top commenters. Names of people she knew. Coworkers and casual friends. Even her ex-husband. *Sympathies... So tragic... Will miss her... explains work absence...* Who were they talking about? Heart in her throat, she clicked on the linked news vid dated shortly after midnight. It showed an apartment building assaulted by a raging inferno, flames punching from the windows in the five-story brownstone like the fires of hell. The firefighters struggled to contain it. The surrounding buildings were familiar, but not the one aflame. That one was unrecognizable... given the location, it should be—*Shit!* It was *her* apartment building! Her stunned brain barely registered the streaming text tied to the video, catching only random words. *All dead... Preditech employee... body confirmed... no immediate family... dead...*

Eve jackknifed to her feet, shaking and heaving for air, drowning in shock. Her apartment building had caught fire last night, and had burned to the ground? And no one had survived? Of all the people who had lived there, she was the only one still alive? But she'd been pronounced dead as well? Not assumed dead, but confirmed dead. That meant somebody—*some body*—had been found in her home and nobody had questioned whether it was her body?

As far as the world was concerned, she was dead.

The looming stacks of books closed in on her like giant

fingers to crush a bug. The calm air mocked her, refusing to be drawn into her lungs. Her throat burned, as if filled with caustic smoke, and all warmth drained from her body. She was dead. As certainly as MadDog in the alley. As surely as the cyborg on the street today. Murdered. Dead. Gone.

Alone.

Eve clamped a hand over her mouth to keep from screaming, hot tears streaming from her eyes so she could barely see. She grabbed her purse and ran toward the door. Betty called to her, but Eve didn't hear the words and couldn't stop her momentum out of the library and down the street, blind to where she headed because it no longer mattered. She was dead.

Chapter Fifteen

Adam circled the area as best he could, given the fact the area's streets contoured with the deep curve of the nearby White River rather than lay in a proper grid. Too many one-ways and curves and dead ends to make his search easy.

Didn't matter. He still scoured the neighborhood, scanning for Eve in an ever-widening path from the strangled mass of metal and glass he figured was her car. The pile would likely have fit her description, if someone hadn't demolished it. What remained of her vehicle looked similar to the destruction wrought by the cyborg in Chicago. Were there two rogue cyborgs? Had someone used the idea as a diversion to kidnap Eve? Had someone tried to kill her again?

Had they succeeded?

He'd slowly driven past the car, his muscles tensed and his scanners primed, but there was no evidence of a struggle. The area enjoyed a steady flow of people out for Sunday dinner, so any abduction or attempted murder would have had a witness. The police would have been called, but there was no sign of any crime scene investigation.

Everything seemed perfectly normal for a weekend evening.

He was probably being paranoid—pretty typical for him, really —thinking something was wrong with Eve. He couldn't prove that pile of metal was her car, and if she had decided to stay, why hadn't she come looking for him?

Oh, right. Maybe because he'd walked away from her. Yes, he'd had his reasons, and they still stood… he wasn't safe for anyone to be around. But he couldn't delete from his memory the look of hurt on her face when she'd finally emerged from his bedroom, dressed and ready to leave. Guilt had smacked him upside the head for being the cause of that wounded expression, and he'd wanted to enfold her in his arms, promise her the moon and stars, and kiss her until she smiled again. He'd resisted the urge. Barely. Offering such little white lies contradicted his officer's training, and aside from his physiological reaction as a man to a beautiful woman, his interest in Eve was purely professional. Sure, he was technically no longer an officer of the law. But he had taken an oath to uphold the public trust and hold people accountable for their actions and all that. So his concern for her had nothing to do with the little flutter in his heart whenever he looked at her.

While he couldn't lie to Eve, he was apparently okay with lying to himself.

The quiver in his belly and tension in his shoulders as he drove around searching for her was more than mere professional concern for her safety because he was still a cop at heart. But he'd known her less than twenty-four hours. A person—much less a cyborg with a mechanical heart—couldn't develop tender feelings for another in such a short period of time. Love took months. Years, even. The tight ache in his chest had to be heartburn. Or coronary failure.

Yet it felt like so much more.

His volatile heartbeats and touchy Spidey-senses were becoming the new normal since he'd met Eve. He shouldn't have taken her home last night. He shouldn't have left her alone this morning. He shouldn't have kissed her this afternoon. She was a danger to the life he'd established. A threat to the droning familiarity of his meaningless existence. He should have no interest in her secret information. He should have no concern for her well-being and safety. She was a grown woman and had proved she was smart and capable.

Damn it all to hell, he shouldn't have sent her away. His fancy cybernetic mainframe couldn't compute why he was so concerned about her, and he didn't have time to figure it out. Not with his heart pounding and his lower back tingling like a pneumatic nail gun. Every nanonerve-muscle graft screamed she needed him.

Until he found her, or evidence of her, he would continue to search. Not like he had anything better to do. He drove through the surrounding neighborhoods, his ever-widening sweep taking him past the original Broad Ripple Village boundaries and into the Greater Broad Ripple area which had been annexed several decades ago. His gaze swept in constant arcs for a sign of her or her whereabouts. As the shadows lengthened toward evening, he spotted a lone figure in a black suit jacket and designer heels shuffling and stumbling like a zombie along the uneven concrete sidewalk in a neglected neighborhood.

The tension in his shoulders evaporated as he pulled up next to her and jumped out, sliding across the front of his car to get to her before she could run away or break an ankle in those heels on that cracked sidewalk.

"Eve." He breathed her name as he grasped her shoulders. She blinked at his chest, her gaze unfocused and her expression shell-shocked. A gentle shake and she blinked again. Lifting her gaze to his face, her eyes widened in recognition.

She clutched his shirt as a sob tore loose from her throat. "I'm dead, Adam. They killed me."

The words speared his heart with alarm, and he ignored the wave of relief which washed over him now that she was back in his arms. She was obviously alive, so claiming someone had killed her made no sense. He would dig deeper for its meaning, but at the moment, he thanked the Maker she was uninjured. Tucking her to his side, he walked her to the idling car and eased her to the seat. There, that was nothing special. He'd put lots of individuals into a squad car in much the same way. However, he hadn't then reached in and buckled their seatbelts for them, like he did Eve. And he hadn't given their knee a tender squeeze before closing the door, like he did Eve.

He stood and clenched his fists, berating his own idiocy. Okay, fine, he cared about her. He could admit it. But this wasn't about him. She needed comfort, and they needed a safe place to talk.

He slid around to his side and drove away.

She rocked in her seat, her hand over her mouth as if to keep her sorrow, or her lunch, from spewing forth. Of their own volition, his fingers sought out her other hand and clasped it, his thumb rubbing across the tops of her knuckles.

He drove with no destination in mind, but ended in his own driveway. His house might not be the safest choice, what with visits from old partners and attempted break-ins. Someone might be casing it, and he'd pulled up with Eve clearly visible in the passenger seat. But it was his home. It was familiar territory and it held his gun. Adam pulled Eve out of the car and steered her into the house and directly to the living room. She walked like an automaton, wooden yet compliant, quiet tears streaming down her cheeks as he sat her on the couch, removed her suit jacket and eased off her heels. The moment he cupped her shapely calf muscle, desire slammed him. His hands shook with the urge to spread those long legs wide and lose himself in the heaven at their apex. His gaze traveled up her thighs to where their creamy length met the edge of his borrowed shirt. His cock hardened in his pants, like she was true north and he the compass.

She was distraught, thinking someone had killed her, and

here he was getting chubbed over bits of exposed skin like a fucking adolescent. She deserved better. He bit the inside of his cheek and leaned forward far enough the crease of his pants pinched his dick. The dual pain tempered his desire.

Gently lifting her hand in his right hand, his cyborg hand grasping the edge of the coffee table just in case it glitched, he rubbed her knuckles and cleared his throat to pull her head out of whatever nightmare she was reliving.

"Eve, talk to me. What the hell do you mean you're dead?" He kept his voice low and soft. She looked so small and vulnerable sitting there, her head bent in defeat, still rocking. Why would anyone want her dead? What could she have done that was so bad she'd been marked?

She pulled her hand from his and blinked. Her eyes lost their unfocused haze, like a frozen computer that had finally finished processing its tsunami of commands and could proceed again as normal. She frowned. "Wh-what do you mean?"

It was his turn to blink. "I found you wandering a neighborhood a mile from where I'd dropped you off, and you claimed you were dead. That *they killed you*. What did you mean?"

"I said that?" She shook her head, either to clear it or to deny what she'd said. "Not sure why I'd say anyone killed me. I mean, I'm right here, aren't I?" She huffed a hollow laugh and rolled her eyes in a self-depreciating manner. "Must be the exhaustion talking. They killed *him*. You know, MadDog. They killed MadDog."

She clasped his hand "Adam, why aren't you at work? You didn't get fired, did you?"

Classic denial, deflection, and distraction, that's what she was doing. Unfortunately for her, he'd seen those tactics used by masters. Her amateur attempt was as transparent as a vodka bottle. He could play the game for now.

"I'm not fired. It was a slow night and my boss let me take off." Her mouth puckered into an adorable O. He licked his lips and focused his attention away from all the places he wanted to caress and kiss. "I saw your car. Did you?"

Her shoulders slumped. "Yes. Right before… right before I started walking around." She shrugged. "Didn't know what else to do."

"You aren't upset your car was destroyed?"

She gasped. "Hell yes, I'm upset! I just sent in the final payment! Now I'm stuck here with no car. I can't even return home because"—She gulped and her gaze darted to the side—"Obviously because I have no car. No car, no phone, no—uh, no money, right? It would probably be a bad idea to use my credit cards, right?"

Nodding, Adam rested his elbows on his thighs and let the silence ring. Let her work through whatever she was mentally wrangling with and, dare he hope, let her grow uncomfortable enough in the lull of conversation to unwittingly divulge useful information. Silence was a common interrogation technique cops used because it worked well on all but the most hardened criminals. He didn't have to wait long.

"Look, um, Adam." She stared at her toes. "I know you don't really know me. And I know helping me kinda put you in a tight spot with the police. And you don't want—I mean, you've already done so much for me that I hate to ask you for more. But…" She cleared her throat and raised her warm-toffee gaze to his. Pleading desperation shimmered in their depths. Hopelessness bracketed her lips. "Could I please stay with you another night or two? Until, um… until I can figure out what else to do?"

She sat, every muscle tensed and waiting his answer, like she stood before a firing line of one and he held the rifle. Her lips didn't rub together like when she was nervous. Instead, they formed a thin, expectant line like she assumed he would deny her request. Was her situation so damn dire that a simple answer from him could make or break her?

"Of course you can, Eve." He couldn't tell her *no* any more than his body could keep from yearning to feel her soft skin. A ridiculous reaction since he couldn't act on his desire. The little episode in the bedroom this afternoon proved his glitching parts were a danger to her.

Relief whooshed from her and her lips lifted in a hesitant smile. "Thank you. I don't know who else to ask."

Her comment made no sense. Surely she had someone else she could turn to besides a practical stranger she'd met last night in a bar. "What about family? Friends? Do you have anyone still in Chicago you could get in contact with?"

Blood fled her face and her expression turned bleak, her eyes glassy and focused inward. She shook her head, her lips trembling, and her voice a rough whisper. "They killed everyone. They set the entire building on fire. Nobody survived. Not even me."

She made no sense, but people in shock rarely did. He continued to rub her hand and speak in a low, nonthreatening voice. "When did they do this?"

"Last night. Actually, early this morning." Her gaze jerked to his. "Not too long after MadDog died. They either knew they'd failed, or this was part of a multipronged plan to erase me. Maybe the attempted break-in this morning was also part of their plan. Then my car."

She sounded like a street prophet looking directly into the void of the end of the world. If he hadn't seen MadDog die in her arms and witnessed the drone, if his gut didn't tell him the cops were interested in her for more than information on MadDog, he might have waved off her comments as mere garden-variety ramblings. But her concern was valid, and he believed her. "So, someone set an apartment on fire—"

"My apartment. My home in Chicago, The whole building."

"—okay, your apartment. And everyone died, including you?"

"Yes." She nodded with such vigor, her braids unraveled.

"They've claimed I'm dead. Confirmed the body and publicly announced my death."

"How did they confirm your body, if you're here with me and alive?"

"I don't know, but it's on the news." She shrugged, her gaze darting around the room as if she were looking for something. Her breath hitched. "If I'm dead, I can't do anything. I can't access my bank accounts. Can't use my credit cards. Can't drive anywhere. Can't buy a car. I have no resources."

Adam chuffed her forearms, daring to use both hands to comfort her. "Do you think they realize it's not your body they found? Or do you think they planted the body there?" When she shrugged, he continued. "Eve. Who is this *they* we're talking about?"

Again she shrugged. And choked back a sob. He canted his head to catch her gaze. "I've told you before, and I'll say it again. I can't help you if you don't talk to me."

Eve nodded, pulling her arms away to wrap around her torso. She swallowed, rocked, and inhaled deeply before she whispered as if his house was bugged. "It's my employer."

"Preditech?"

She nodded.

"Does this have anything to do with the corporate corruption information you say you have?"

She nodded again.

"We're talking more than proof they cheated on their taxes or bribed government officials, aren't we."

She nodded once more. He waited for her to confess, letting the silence ring uncomfortably.

"Th-they killed him." Her breath hitched and she finally lifted her gaze to his. She mushed her lips together and drew in a deep breath. "They killed him like he was a rabid dog."

She had proof her employer was involved in murdering MadDog? A death that was meant for her? His cop's intuition didn't believe it was true. She lacked the desperation, the panic, of someone fleeing a death mark. He reached his right hand out to tuck an errant strand of her rich auburn hair behind her ear. "Look, I'm sure MadDog understood the risks—"

She shook her head so the strand worked its way out again, her voice thick with emotion. "I'm not talking about him. I mean the cyborg on the news."

Her face crumpled and she dropped her head in her hands and sobbed. Adam blinked back his shock. *They killed him like he was a rabid dog.* She cried for the brutal death of a cyborg when the rest of the world had cheered. She shed tears for a man she hadn't known. Awed by her admission—such a dangerous opinion to have in these times—Adam shifted from the coffee table to the couch and lifted her onto his lap. He wrapped his arm around her, rubbing her back, either to offer her comfort or to convince himself she was real. Perhaps a bit of both.

Would she cry for him?

She turned her face into his shoulder as he stroked her back. His mouth opened, but no words emerged. What could he possibly say? Life was unfair, and every cyborg knew their life was meaningless. Worthless. Society could barely be bothered to strip them for the cost of their cybernetic parts, much less care about them as living creatures. Seeing one murdered reminded him he couldn't fight his fate. Adam wished he could tell her everything would be okay, but he couldn't lie to her, even to assuage her sorrow.

He could only offer himself as a pathetic substitute. "Eve, tell me what you need."

"They... they killed him." She stuttered against his chest. She had wrapped her arms around his torso, and grasped his shirt, holding him as if she could burrow inside and find safety there. Adam yearned to promise it to her, even though it might not be true. She spoke through her sobs. "They're going to kill them all. They know it, and they can fix it, but they're not trying.

They won't. They'll just hide the truth and let them die. I have to do something. I have to save them. I have to tell people what's going on."

"What is Preditech doing to cyborgs, darlin'?"

She pulled back as if shot, her eyes wide and her expression fearful. She opened her mouth, no doubt to deny the truth, but dropped her head back to his chest and sighed instead.

"The power electrodes grafted to the microchips in the CPU are substandard and deteriorate over time, interrupting internet protocol to the modem so automated software updates get corrupted. And the corrupted updates can result in violent system malfunctions."

So basically, Adam had a bad motivator?

"Why are you telling me this now, when I've asked before?"

"Because this time you called me *darlin'*." Her voice was petulant, like she couldn't decide if she was pleased or not with the endearment. If it got her to open up to him, he'd use the it all the time.

Adam pulled her back to look in her eyes. "Someone seriously doesn't want this information getting out."

"Of course not. It would destroy Preditech's reputation, and they have extensive corporate and government contracts."

"It's possible this is bigger than Preditech. Someone burned an entire apartment complex with Chicago firefighters on the scene, to either kill you or fake your death. Someone destroyed your car beyond recognition, but left your phone on the dash. And a military-issue drone tried to kill you with a deadly, experimental virus. Eve—darlin'—someone is willing to go to great lengths to make sure no one finds out what you know."

She frowned, the off-centered crease between her eyes deep with concern. "When was there a drone with a deadly virus? Why would you say that?"

"Well, before you went searching on trigger-sensitive websites with my computer, I did a little looking myself.

MadDog was likely killed by a mutated virus the government is working on. And that fun little virus was delivered via drone. I saw it in the alley while you were distracted by his death."

She stared at him for several moments, obviously debating. Should she believe him? Should she trust him? Should she run away? He waited patiently until she made her decision. Finally, she canted her head to the side, her face pinched with confusion. "What are the odds I'd walk into a bar with a bouncer who happens to know where to find that kind of information."

"More to the point, what are the odds you'd walk into a bar with a bouncer who used to be a cop."

Crap, that detail had slipped out. Eve stiffened and pulled away from him, her eyes like saucers. "You said I couldn't trust the cops. Yet you're one of them."

Adam shook his head, regretting that he'd opened that can of worms. "Used to be. I'm not anymore. I'm a bouncer."

She crossed her arms over her chest, but didn't retreat. Hopefully that was a good sign. Her side glance was guarded. "Once a cop, always a cop. Isn't that what they say?"

If only. Bitterness seeped into his voice. "You're thinking of Marines. Look, a former officer of the law could conceivably maintain the personality traits which qualified him to be a good cop in the first place. But once the badge is retired, there's no guarantee he stays part of the fraternity."

Her wary expression melted into concern. She braced a hand on his shoulder, turning to better face him. "What happened? Why did they turn their back on you?"

Her compassion nearly undid him. He squeezed her thigh where his good hand rested. "Let's just say I made a wrong decision. And I've had to live with the fallout ever since."

She cocked her head to the side, contemplating him as if he'd offered her a piece of a puzzle she was working on. "Is this decision also why your fiancée left you?"

Too damn perceptive. He nodded.

She returned his nod. "If we live long enough, we all make mistakes we regret. You regret the decision which made your fellow officers turn on you. Maybe your fiancée regrets leaving you."

"She probably regrets not leaving me sooner. So what's your regret?"

He expected her to say finding the Preditech secret or walking into his bar. But her gaze lowered to where his hand lay on her lap. She mushed her lips together. "Thinking I can make the world a better place. That I can help fix the broken parts. I'm only one person and it's such a big world."

She lifted her gaze, but stopped at his lips. "But it brought me here. To this moment. This might also be a mistake, but I doubt I'll regret it."

His brain blue-screened as she kissed him.

Chapter Sixteen

Eve wasn't normally the sexual aggressor, not that this kiss was anything more than tentative. Still, he didn't kiss her back. Why would he? He'd walked away from her this morning when she'd been nearly naked and definitely willing. When he'd been ignorant of the baggage she carried. When she hadn't truly known him. Had wrongfully assumed what kind of man he was.

She pulled away. "I'm… I'm sorry."

"No, don't be sorry." A flash of panic raced across Adam's face and his voice held a sliver of desperation. "You surprised me, is all."

Truth be told, she'd surprised herself. Confessing her secret to him was a relief, like lifting the world off her shoulders. Funny how the weight of responsibility for one little mini-drive was a thousand-fold its actual mass. Or maybe this was less about removing the weight entirely, but sharing the burden with someone else. Someone strong and capable. Someone she hoped she could trust.

Someone who wasn't what she'd pigeonholed him to be.

"Don't stop. I'm over my initial shock." His hand at her back pressed her closer and his lips lifted in a grin so wickedly handsome, her core clenched and she caught her breath. His gaze dropped to her lips. "You won't be sorry this time."

He'd misunderstood her apology. Eve lifted her hand to his cheek, loving the slight rough texture of his stubble. "I wasn't apologizing for the kiss. I meant, I'm sorry I assumed you were a simple bar bouncer with rap sheet and a troubled past."

"I *am* a simple bar bouncer with a rap sheet and a troubled past." He leaned in for a kiss.

Eve pulled back and frowned at him. "You have a rap sheet?"

His grin turned impish and his shoulders hitched in a half-shrug. "I have a few parking tickets I'm late paying."

"Oooh, such a hardened criminal." She snickered, but it ended with a needy sigh. She reevaluated her attraction. Bad boys with tattoos had always been her weakness, not that she'd ever had the nerve or the opportunity to date one. But the cowboy type with the southern drawl which stripped away any reservations with a single *darlin'* also made her insides quiver. And who didn't love the promise of protection from a first responder?

And she'd been hot for him before. Lava ran through her veins, burning from the inside out so her body fairly vibrated with need. She tipped her forehead to his, her voice thick with desire. "Adam, please tell me now if you have groceries to put away or expect a friendly visit from local law enforcement or just aren't that into me." She drew a deep breath, his campfire-bourbon-metal scent filling her nose and lungs. "Because I want you. I want you to… I want to…"

She swallowed, her nerve evaporating, unable to say how much she wanted to be with him. To…

"Fuck me." Adam groaned as if it was his last breath, a completion of her thought, a statement of his own. A declaration of surrender.

He whispered her name as a reverent prayer and kissed her. Deep. Desperate. His tongue dancing against hers, his lips caressing. The magma in her veins erupted, and she moaned in his mouth, squirming on his lap, running her hands over his arms and shoulders. Needed their strength. Wanted their support as she careened through a cloud of desire.

"Fuck." Adam breathed and twisted so she rested against the couch back. Her hips tilting with the new angle of her body, her legs falling open against his thigh and the hem of her shirt riding up hers. The relative chill of the room whispered against the crotch of her panties, offering a degree of relief from the building heat. His lips walked a searing trail of kisses along her jaw to her ears and down her neck. The arm behind her reached around and fingers fumbled with the buttons of her shirt.

Before Eve could offer to help, Adam grunted in frustration, grasped the fabric, and tore it open. Buttons pinged where they flew across the room. He didn't blink at the destruction of his clothing, instead swooping down to pull a lace-covered breast into his hungry mouth, sucking and licking the mound and scraping his teeth across the taut nipple.

Sheets of need rained from her breasts down to her toes and she moaned.

Hating the thin barrier of her bra, Eve yanked at the straps, the cups peeling away from Adam's hot mouth. With renewed vigor, his attention volleyed between each breast and his hand slid between her legs, pausing as if expecting her to stop him. When she answered his unspoken question by pushing her pelvis against his hand, he wriggled his fingers beneath the fabric barrier and laid claim to her slick folds and needy entrance, spreading her arousal and circling her clit before delving into her aching core and repeating the path until she thought she might die.

Eve reached between their bodies to find the bulge of his erection pressing against his jeans. Palming the thick outline, she stroked the length and cupped the bulge of his testicles.

"Fuck, I gotta taste you." Adam growled as he slid out from

under her and off the couch, shoved at the coffee table so it tipped over, and tugged her hips to the edge of the couch. She planted her heels against his back as he yanked her panties to the side and buried his face between her thighs. This was no tender seduction. He was a starving man at a buffet, ravishing her with his tongue, teeth, and lips. Eve had never been so manhandled, and by a man who toed the line of control. It set her on fire. She clawed at the couch and the muscled forearm resting beside her hips. She arched and rocked, grinding against Adam's mouth as his tongue lapped at her clit and thrust into her core until her body quivered and her moans and panting breaths filled the quiet Sunday evening like a gospel chorus in an empty church.

He slid two fingers deep inside and sucked hard on her clit, blasting her up and over the edge of her orgasm. Eve cried out, her body lurching as the power of her release thrashed her like waves against the rocky shore. She trembled. Stars winked behind her eyelids. Her breathe seized in her lungs.

She wanted more.

"Eve." Her name a demand, Adam heaved her into his arms, her legs wrapped around his torso, and marched toward his bedroom, ravishing her mouth and shedding his clothes along the way. Eve clawed at his shirt, needing to see that magnificent chest again, to feel the muscles ripple beneath her fingertips. He turned and anchored her against the hallway wall with his hips, the cold metal of his dangling belt buckle teasing the underside of her ass, the bulge of his erection pressing against her belly, and angled his upper half back so he could toss the damn shirt off.

She clutched his chest, scraping her nails over his puckered brown nipples, running her fingers through his chest hair, tracing the contours of his abdominal muscles which flinched at her greedy touch.

"Eve." A warning.

"Fuck me." A plea.

He whirled her around and into his bedroom, dropping her onto the mattress and following her down. The heat of his skin flush with hers, his weight pressing against her, his kisses stealing her conscious thought. His was the intensity she'd always yearned for. It called to her, beckoned her to lose herself, to set aside sanity and propriety and responsibility and simply *be*.

Adam lifted his weight and leaned forward, rummaging in a nightstand drawer. He pulled back, kneeling between her legs with something in his hand, but her attention caught on his beautiful cock standing full and proud, jutting toward her, it's rosy head glistening and a bead of pre-cum clinging like a tear of joy. She wanted to wrap her hands around its girth. Wanted to run her tongue along its velvety length, let it stretch her jaw as she sucked it into her mouth. Wanted to buck and thrust it deep inside her pulsing core. Wanted—

"Fuck." A curse. Eve pulled her gaze from Adam's cock. He scowled at something in his hand. A misshapen, crackled puck of whitish rubber. A condom, or what had once been one. He caught her gaze and pursed his lips, waving the dried-out prophylactic and its gold wrapper. "It's a little out of date."

Looking more disappointed than a child whose candy had been stolen, he tossed the unusable condom away. When he turned back, his smile was once again wicked as he slid her panties off. "But that means I get to lick you some more."

Before he could reposition, Eve grasped his cock and gently stroked from base to bulbous tip. His eyelids fluttered closed and he sucked in a breath with a loud hiss. She wrapped her legs around his hips and tightened, pulling him closer to situate his head at her entrance, already slick with his saliva and her own juices.

Propped on her elbow, Eve ran a hand over his hip and around, gripping a powerful buttock. She squeezed her legs to pull him closer, further inside, but he resisted her. A desperate whimper gurgled in her throat.

"Adam, I have a contraceptive implant and I'm clean. From the look of things, I'm guessing you're clean too." She nodded in the direction of the discarded condom. Rolling her hips, which nudged his head further inside. Adam moaned low and fell forward, bracing his weight on his hands. He kissed her long and deep before coming up for air. Gazing at her, his pupils wide and dark, he shook his head. "I don't have any diseases. But what I want to do to you isn't clean. Fact, it's fucking impure."

Eve smiled and stretched out on the bed, her arms out to the side and her knees as wide as she could spread them. An offering. An invitation. A challenge. "Good. Because I want it hard and dirty."

With a throaty growl, Adam plunged his length inside her until his pelvis smacked her thighs, filling her and stretching her so she gasped at the rightness of it. His hips pistoned, his cock thrusting deep inside and retreating at a relentless pace. She gasped and wailed, her entire body lurching on the sheets, her small breasts rocking, the headboard drumming the wall.

Adam fucked her like an animal, owned her body and commanded her pleasure, and damn it was exactly what she wanted. She dug her heels into the mattress and scraped her nails along the straining muscles of his back, desperate to find purchase so she could meet his thrusts with her own. Her hungry core clenched at him, begging for the delicious slide of his length and the heat of that friction. He didn't deny her, and her body melted into a single flame of growing need.

The air filled with the creak of the bedframe and their labored breaths, their moans and primal grunts. Like a rogue tidal wave, Eve's orgasm smashed against her with breathtaking force, crashing her into the mattress and ripping screams from her hoarse throat, one lengthy "Fuuuuuuuuuck!" as the explosion of pleasure electrocuted her until she collapsed, quivering and spent.

Vaguely aware of Adam roaring his own release and then covering her in a boneless, panting heap. As her senses flickered back online, like she was a computer rebooting, Adam rolled off of her, pulling her with him so she sprawled across his right side, their arms and legs entwined. Eve molded her body to his, resting her cheek in the soft crook of his shoulder. She gasped for air and swallowed against a parched throat made sore from her screams of release.

Adam wiped at the sweat on his brow and hugged her with one arm. "Ughn. Holy fuck." A prayer for strength. A grunt of gratitude. A punchline.

Eve chuckled softly as sleep crept up her body, from her toes to her consciousness until she drifted away on a sweet cloud of satisfaction.

Chapter Seventeen

Adam waited until his heartbeat calmed to normal and Eve drifted to sleep. Her muscles hiccupped as she crested the hill into slumber and her breathing shifted to a soft whisper.

How he wanted to follow her. Wanted to float from this dreamy after-sex euphoria into a deep, peaceful slumber made all the more serene because such a beautiful, compassionate woman had desired him and now rested in his arms. But fear kept him awake. Fear he might glitch and hurt her. Fear she'd learn what he was and hate him. Fear she'd notice just how close she came to dying tonight.

He pulled his hand away from the silky skin of her back long enough to place a pillow over the section of mattress where his cyborg fingers had torn through the fitted sheet and shredded the mattress beneath. Fucking Eve had been the most intense sex he'd had in, well, ever, causing his cybernetic systems to flicker like a strobe light. Yet even in the hottest moments—and sweet baby Jesus, there had been so many—he'd thankfully had the presence of mind to keep his left hand away from her. He still couldn't see out of his eye, and his heart stuttered on occasion. If his systems failed completely, with her sated and sleeping beside him, it would be the most pleasant way to go. But until then, he worried what havoc his systems could wreak on Eve.

He'd be damned if he'd let a glitch so much as bruise her luscious body, but that was the thing about glitches, wasn't it? He couldn't control or predict them. So he'd lived with the constant worry an essential system would falter in a public arena and people would know what he was. Now, that worry escalated into sheer terror he would hurt Eve. Memories of the rogue cyborg from the afternoon shredding cars morphed into images of Adam ripping away pieces of Eve's body—

He flinched, biting his tongue to keep from yelling at the horror. So much for after-sex bliss.

Easing off the bed so he didn't wake her, he took one last peek of her glorious body—fighting the urge to take her tender breasts into his mouth again—before covering her with a blanket. He retrieved his pants from the hall and wandered to the kitchen. Through the window over the kitchen sink, the sun's final rays lingered in the night sky, although it felt like midnight. His life was normally filled with mere passing human interaction and less excitement. The past twenty-four hours had been rife with both, but he wasn't sure it was a bad thing? His life had jumped the rails since Eve had walked into his bar, but that little morsel of heaven was also asleep in his bed. The tingle in the small of his back told him there would be more of everything.

More of Eve could make it all worthwhile. Hopefully she returned the sentiment.

His stomach rumbled the need for food, so he made a sandwich and fussed with the broken hardware of his cabinet while he chewed, pulling the bent screws and removing the snapped hinges but leaving the door off. He meandered over to his computer to check out the security system Eve had suggested might have been bypassed. He reviewed the security feed, and sure enough, two men circled the house, no doubt trying to find a way in while he'd been at the police station and she'd been unprotected. Why hadn't his entry-point alarms pinged him? Yes, his system was old school, but that shouldn't mean it was as derelict as he was.

Shit! The men pulled a hand-held device from a back pocket. Their grainy image on the monitor screen grew staticky each time one tested the lock of an entry point, then cleared when they moved on. Adam looked more closely. Each time the static hit, the man holding the device pressed it. Damn. Apparently, his old-school system had been jammed, which explained why he hadn't received an alarm ping.

When the men reached the garage door, the one not holding the jammer pulled what looked to be a micro-tablet from his pocket, his fingers flying over the screen. The garage door lifted on its motorized chain. The men walked in as if they owned the place.

Sonuvabitch! Adam's muscles clenched and his vision ran red. His entire security system had been rendered useless with a couple low-tech devices. But the most enraging part of this was the fact Eve had been in the house at the time. Alone. Helpless. The men could have hurt her. Could have done unimaginable things to her, and he wouldn't have known until hours later. Some fucking former officer he was. As if being around his glitching cyborg parts didn't put her in enough physical danger, these men could have killed her. Could have—

The men ran out of the garage, terrified, shoving at each other as if chased by a monster. Or a ferocious dog. Adam smiled. Eve had mentioned scaring them away. So, she wasn't helpless, and he shouldn't have underestimated her wily self-preservation skills. Maybe the key to his home security was going even older school than his current system. Maybe he needed to invest in a large guard dog.

"I didn't mean to fall asleep." Eve's soft confession pulled his attention from the security screen. He swiveled in his chair to see her standing at the wide entrance to the room wearing another one of his shirts, the collar hanging at an angle off her slender shoulders and the hem skimming mid-thigh—no sweats this time, so the delicious length of leg was bare, much to his delight—her hair delightfully disheveled. Rumpled and well-fucked. She should always look like that.

She leaned against the doorframe, hugging herself as if self-conscious, and stared at the couch and the coffee table still listing on its side. A soft flush crept up her throat and she licked her lips, no doubt remembering what they'd done in this room a couple hours ago. Blood surged to Adam's cock at the memory and the vision in front of him. He licked his lips. "No need to apologize. You haven't had much sleep."

"Neither have you, and you didn't doze off. Guess I'm not used to such a"—she cleared her throat—"strenuous workout."

Neither was he. Bar patrons often made comments alluding to what they assumed was his active sex life. But he didn't have one. The proof of how not-active his sex life was rested on his nightstand.

"If you're looking for a workout partner to help you build your stamina…" He pointed at himself. "I recommend starting with a set of several reps. Take a short breather, and doing another set."

She giggled, her blush deepening. She pushed off the wall to straighten the room, righting the table, folding clothes, retrieving scattered buttons. He nearly came in his pants each time she bent, his shirt riding up to right under her lush backside. He knew what she tasted like there. He knew the heat of her core when he was buried deep inside her. He knew the throaty tone of her cries of release. They still rang in his ears, just as the scrapes still tingled where she'd clawed his back. She hadn't been a demure, passive lover like he'd assumed she would be, even as he'd found his haven within the circle of her arms and thighs. No, she'd been bold. Demanding. Meeting him thrust for thrust.

Sex with her had been hot enough to melt his wires. And the memory made him hard as stone again.

"Are those the guys who tried to break in earlier today?" She nodded toward the monitor where he'd paused the security recording. She looked back to her fascinating task. Why was she avoiding looking at him?

Adam cleared his throat and willed his erection to go away. "Yeah. They overrode my security with some sort of jamming device. They weren't able to override my entry-point locks, but they did get the garage door up. You were smart to scare them away like you did."

"Or maybe just lucky." She shrugged as if she didn't believe it.

"Why can't you be both?" She paused, her back to him. He leaned forward to better pinch the tip of his rebellious cock. And to be closer to her. "Your idea to stream angry dogs barking was ingenious. And luckily worked."

She turned, high heels and a folded shirt clutched to her chest like armor, her gaze toward the window but not focused on it. "They'll be back. Won't they?"

He nodded. "Most likely. And will be prepared for a big dog."

She settled on the arm of the couch and brought her gaze to his. Angry tears shimmered at the edges of her eyes. "Or they're already here."

Adam's gaze swerved to his security screen and clicked the live feed, his muscles tensed for a fight. He'd secure Eve in a closet and grab his gun and—

The screen was empty. Nothing. No intruders. No suspicious shadows. He turned back to her, eyebrows raised in question.

Her lips thinned to a mulish frown. "Not out there. In here. Someone to offer me safety and concern. Someone to pretend to be my friend."

She thought *he* was one of *them*? That he worked with the

people trying to kill her? His blood boiled at the false accusation. He'd gone above and beyond the call of a duty which wasn't his anymore because he was no longer a badge. He was in the crosshairs of an enemy he didn't know because he couldn't just leave her alone and in danger.

He inhaled to counter her accusation, but she wasn't finished. She continued enumerating his alleged crimes. "You saw a drone no one else did. You just happen to know about an experimental viral warfare cocktail used to kill MadDog. Your employer just happened to give you the night off." She jolted to her feet and plunked her fists on her hips, the clothes tumbling to the floor, forgotten, as the motor revved on the stupid-as-fuck-and-completely-wrong conspiracy theory about him. "You just happened to offer me sanctuary when anyone else would have wished me luck and sent me on my way. You just happened to get called to the police station before two men could try to break in and get the mini-drive I carry, or kill me, or both. And you just happened to fuck my brains out so I'd fall in love with you and do whatever you say and never suspect you of a damn thing. You're their spy, their secret weapon, right? Their way to lure me to my own doom."

Her voice pitched higher as she spoke until she sounded like a tea kettle. It reminded him of her passionate cries when she'd reached her climax, but the content of her words enraged him. He lurched to his feet, grasping the chair's back as it rolled away. Outrage and grief warred in his chest. He'd failed to defend his innocence when his fellow cops had immediately assumed his cybernetic implants meant he would become a crazed robot and menace to the force. He'd be damned if he'd fail to clear his name with Eve.

But his gut countered with the possibility there was more to this outburst. More to why Eve laid such horrid accusations at his feet. She was terrified. Like a wounded animal, lashing out at those who sought to help.

He inhaled a calming breath and focused on her instead of his roiling emotions. "So… what I hear you say is you've fallen in love with me."

That shocked her to a dead stop in her tirade. "Wh-what?"

"You said I fucked your brains out. I won't lie, darlin', you fucked my brains out in return. And I wouldn't mind another go at it. Or two. But you also said you'd fallen in love with me. I'm honored, as that hasn't happened often, even with my sparkling personality and this—" He waved his right hand to indicate his body.

She blinked and wrapped her arms around her torso. She spoke carefully, obviously weighing her words this time. "I-I didn't say I'd actually fallen in love with you. I meant that you're under orders to fuck me so I'll think I'm in love and will trust you so they can get to me."

"Well, since you're not in love with me, I must be a pretty shitty spy. Or bad in bed. I blame any performance issues on the stress of my assignment. I mean, James Bond couldn't make a woman so completely forget herself that she'd lose all sense of self-preservation, but yet those are apparently my orders."

She frowned, but didn't respond. He continued like they were discussing the weather. "Maybe you'd kindly give me a mulligan and I could try again to fuck your brains out in order to fulfill my so-called orders."

He nodded in the direction of his bedroom. She blinked, turned to look, then swiveled her confused gaze back to his. "You… You're confessing to being a spy?"

"Darlin' if it got me buried balls-deep in you again, I'd say just about anything."

"So…" She cleared her throat, her gaze darting around the room before settling back on his. "So…the sex was that good, huh."

"Best I've ever had. Look, I'd truly hate for something to

happen to you. And honestly, the thought of what *could* happen keeps me awake at night."

He nodded toward the monitor. He hadn't come out and denied his culpability, but hoped his actions proved his innocence more than empty declarations. Hoped he'd talked her off the window ledge before she panicked even more. She hugged herself, mushing her lips together. Her half-chuckle was bitter. "I'm being stupid. You've gone out of your way to help me, and I accuse you of espionage. I'm so sorry, Adam."

"You're scared, I get it. Alone and not knowing who to trust." He stepped toward her, his hands out in supplication. "If I had a corrupt corporation after me, I'd be terrified, too. I can't say—"

She gasped, her gaze focused beside him. Adam looked, and his gut dropped. The chair back he'd been clasping in his left hand was crushed. Frame splintered and cover ripped, metal supports bent. He'd lost control during her tirade, not aware of how hard he gripped the chair, not realizing he'd destroyed it. The good news was it provided unwitting evidence he was not a spy.

The bad news was it proved he was a cyborg.

Chapter Eighteen

The proof before her eyes doused every ember of suspicion Eve had conjured about Adam. The desk chair had been like the rest of his furniture. Solid, sturdy, and well-built, if old. Oak, leather, metal. Yet it had crumpled under his grip as if made of balsa wood, tissue paper, and foil. The destruction eerily similar to the hand-sized hole in his mattress, inches from where she had lain when they'd had sex.

There was no way he was working with Preditech to kill her. He wasn't a spy or a hitman or even an undercover cop. The proof was obvious.

He was a cyborg.

She approached, drawn to him as inexorably as she had from their first meeting, pieces of the puzzle which was Adam at last slipping into place. He saw a drone no one else had. His mismatched blue eyes and the reddish shadow in the left one. A cabinet door ripped from its hinges. The fact he rarely used his left hand, including to touch her. And when he had, how he'd nearly ripped out her hair. That he was no longer an officer. That his fiancée had left him.

Why a man so utterly handsome and potent and considerate lived such a solitary life.

Because, by the miserably ignorant opinion of society, he wasn't a man. He was a machine. A mindless, emotionless mechanical toaster encased in a meat bag.

But she knew better.

"When?" She meant to ask when had he received his cybernetic enhancements, but didn't want to say the words. He was already such a skittish foal about the topic, she didn't want to give him reason to turn away. Hopefully he understood what she was asking.

He frowned at the appendage. "Ten years."

"Alpha-phase?" He nodded. Adam was not only a cyborg, but first-generation. The same generation of cyborg she was trying to save. The odds they would find each other were miniscule, and yet here they were.

Eve reached for his cyborg arm, but Adam twisted away from her. "No." his voice was hoarse, unsettled.

She placed her hand on his chest instead, over his heart. His breath hitched and the muscle flinched where she touched. His hair tickled her fingers, the warmth of his body radiating through her palm and up her arm. His expression was stoic, but his eyes held fear. Fear of hurting her. Fear of how she could hurt him. She only had to say something in a public forum, tell a friend, or hint to a stranger. As if her own situation wasn't equally as precarious.

Her voice low and steady, like comforting a frightened animal. "You are safe with me, Adam. I trust you."

He shook his head to deny it. "No one trusts me."

As an officer of the law, he'd once enjoyed the public's trust. Had fellow officers who had trusted him. The trust and love of a woman. All that had been ripped away from him when he'd received his cybernetic enhancements. "They may not trust your biomechatronic side. But they let you live in peace, don't they?

No one has sent an angry mob to your door. No one has sabotaged your ability to get and keep your current job."

No one has tried to murder you.

A painful lump formed in her throat at the realization her life was even more endangered than a cyborg's. She swallowed, forcing her own self-pity down so she could consider what he'd likely endured. "I've only lived in fear of my life for a few days. I can't begin to imagine what it's been like for you to suffer for years. Worried someone might find out or suspect. Terrified someone will see you and know. Because people hate what they don't understand. And they don't understand you because you exist in between worlds. Not entirely man, and only partially machine."

Eve framed his face with her hands and his right hand encircled her wrist, his left glued at his side. His gaze burned into hers, denial bracketing his mouth, jaws clenched, breathing strained. She ran her thumb along the eyebrow above his cyborg eye. "Either because of your cybernetic parts, or because of the man you are, you're a better human than any of us. That's what makes people so afraid of you. They don't understand the basic fact that these are prosthetics."

"I have more than mere prosthetics, and you know it." He shook his head. "People like their toasters because they push down the button and up pops their toast. But if the toaster could make the choice of whether, when, and how much to toast the bread, people would freak out, throw it away, and replace it with a toaster that works properly. I'm a broken toaster that needs to go in the trash."

"Toasters are sold with the promise that they make toast, period. Not that they'll make better toast than we ever dreamed of and also improve the world in which we live. That's how cybernetic enhancements were marketed. *A Better You,* and all that. But only the end-consumers were targeted, first-responders like you—"

Adam jerked away and stepped back, bumping his desk, his words clipped. "I didn't fall for a marketing campaign or get suckered in by a catchy jingle. I was shot to hell and had a choice: die or get implants. I wasn't ready to die. Thought I had things to live for." He twisted away and stomped toward the hall, his voice filled with bitterness and betrayal. "I was wrong."

Eve flung her body at him, wrapping her arms around his torso and clinging to his back like a dryer sheet to fleece. She held him, her heart weeping for the wrongs he had experienced, as if she could be the armor which protected him from the barbs and arrows of the world outside. Held him with a desperation she'd never before known. He and other cyborgs like him were the reason she had stolen proof of Preditech's corruption. He was the driving factor for why she still sought to get the information into the hands of someone who would do right by it. He was her poster boy, the very personal symbol of her crusade. More importantly, she lov— no, not that. Not yet. She had feelings for him. She… liked him.

She couldn't let him walk away. She had to save him.

"Like I said, you're safe with me." She whispered against his back.

His head hung and he grasped her arms with his right hand like a drowning man clutches a lifeline, his whisper filled with anguish. "But you're not safe with me."

He didn't try to pull away from her, and she didn't move. What was happening to cyborgs made her blood run cold, but his body warmed her. She listened to his quiet breaths. Let his heat seep into her body. Inhaled his familiar scent so it permeated her cells like oxygen. Melted into him until they were one.

If she was a believer in fate, she would know why, of all the bars available, she had walked into his. Mere coincidence wasn't enough to explain why MadDog had chosen The Vogue, and why Adam had helped without being asked, and why she felt more at home with him than she had with any other man.

"Adam, if I wanted to be safe, I would have stayed in Chicago and looked the other way when I found out the truth." She closed her eyes, baring her tender soul. "You think you're a threat, but I've never felt safer in my life than right here with you."

Twisting around in her arms, he threaded fingers through her hair to tilt her face upward. She opened her eyes to meet his stark gaze. Torment flashed across his face. His breath hitched and he swallowed. "I should... I should push you away. Say something cruel so you'll leave and never look back. Whatever it takes to get you far away from here so I can't hurt you. But damn it all, I can't stand the thought of you anywhere but in my arms."

He crushed his lips to hers. She tasted his desperation and pain because she felt them just as potently. And because it was exactly what she needed, what she'd hoped he would offer her. She drowned in his kisses. Returned their fervor with her own powerful need. Teeth clashing and tongues twining, the quiet room filled with their breathless gasps and the growing volume of their moans.

Eve touched everywhere she could reach, delving beneath the waistband of his pants to grip the powerful muscles of his buttocks. Adam mimicked her actions with his broad hands on her ass, squeezing, dipping thick fingers down the cleft to circle in her juices. His erection jutted against her belly. She remembered how beautiful it was, how it filled her and drove her to ecstasy. Remembered how much she wanted to taste it.

While Adam lifted her top, she raised her arms and dropped to her knees, straight out of the shirt. Tugging at the fastener on his pants and pulling them down as she went, she kneeled face-to-face with his cock, hard and seeping. Licking her lips, she gripped him, loving the satiny slide of skin along its rigid length, and flicked her tongue around the head. Adam hissed and moaned, his hips jerking reflexively as she pulled him into her mouth, deeper with each stroke, her tongue swirling around the shaft, her hand massaging his testicles.

Before she could set a rhythm, a loud crunch snapped her out of her reverie.

Adam's left hand had clutched—and cracked—the corner of the couch back. He stared at it, his face mottled with emotion. Hopefully desire. Probably anger. Her gut curdled. He was so afraid to hurt her, to lose control of his hand, that he might use this as an excuse to distance himself from her again. The possibility shot ice through her veins.

He huffed a bleak chuckle and shook his head. "I'm gonna lose a lot of furniture if we keep this up." Despair showered her. He was going to end this before it had gone anywhere. He looked at her, desire still raging in his eyes. Desire, and a wicked glint. "Been meaning to redecorate anyway. Guess I needed a good reason."

What? They were both naked and she'd just had his glorious cock in her mouth, and he wanted to talk home décor? She stood on wobbly knees, "Adam?"

He framed her face with both—both!—hands and kissed her gently. "As much as I loved what you were doing, I need to be inside you more than I need my next breath of air."

His kiss turned deep, demanding. He wrapped an arm around her waist, lifted her, settling her on his cock. They both moaned at the completeness and Eve gripped him with her legs and the hungry walls of her core. As they rocked together, he hurried to the bedroom and laid down with her. He grasped the corner of a pillow with his left hand, no doubt to save his mattress more damage. And to keep her safe.

Eve smiled against his lips and gathered a meager lock of her hair which she held against his hand. "Hold me here, near the ends. If you flinch, you'll only tear a little, but it won't hurt and you'll still be touching me."

His hips paused as he looked at her offering. Slowly, hesitantly, he let go of the pillow and grasped the ends of her hair with his cyborg hand. Fingers which could bring destruction yet could also bring such tender pleasure rubbed the strands like he was touching the silken robes of an angel. Lowering so his torso pressed against hers, he lifted his head so she could gaze into his eyes. Fear evolved into wonder. Wonder to gratitude. Gratitude bloomed into something deeper and more difficult to name, but she was certain her own eyes reflected that same peculiar emotion.

He leaned his weight onto his hands and kissed her again, resuming the magic building where they were connected, but the urgency was gone. In its place was a steadfast tenderness, a merging of bodies which was less about the all-consuming need to reach a mutual pinnacle of pleasure and more about two people whose dreams and desires aligned. A beautiful joining which set her body on fire while it caressed her soul. This was more than sex. This was making love.

When her release crashed upon her, it was all the more intense for the sense of utter completeness filling her. He roared his own release, and she felt it in her heart. Then he rolled her to his side and covered their bodies. She drifted into a sleep more at peace with the universe than she'd ever been.

Chapter Nineteen

Adam woke slowly from a deep, dreamless sleep. He couldn't remember the last time he'd felt so rested and relaxed. The aroma of coffee and bacon filled his nose. Had he died and gone to heaven?

Slipping on a pair of sweats, he padded toward the source of the mouth-watering smell. Eve stood with her back to him, clothed again in little more than one of his shirts—a fashion trend he fully supported—whisking eggs in a bowl while bacon sizzled in a nearby pan. No doubt about it, he *was* in heaven.

And an angel was making him breakfast.

He leaned against the doorframe, the movement catching Eve's attention. She smiled at him, set the bowl down, and walked over. "Hungry?"

His gaze roved the length of her body, from long thoroughbred legs to the paradise beneath the hem of his shirt to her loosely braided hair, and his body reacted as swiftly as a teenage boy in a stiff breeze. Eyes leveled meaningfully at the tight buds of her nipples pointing his direction through the shirt material, he smiled. "Starving."

Her giggle turned to a needy sigh when he pulled her against his chest and covered her mouth in a deep, slow, good-morning kiss. "Me, too." She sighed again and leaned into him, wrapping her arms around his neck. His left hand lay flat and relaxed against her back while his right found its way under the shirt and palmed a luscious mound of her bare ass.

She drew back from the kiss, and patted his shoulders. "I'd better go turn the bacon."

But he couldn't release her. His left arm was locked in place, holding her against him. Grateful the damned appendage didn't flex so she was crushed to his chest or retract so she was thrown across the room, Adam still growled in frustration.

Eve simply smiled and squeezed out to the side, unharmed, her eyes flashing in triumph. And trust. "Coffee is ready and eggs will be in a few. Have a seat."

Adam complied, carefully resting his left arm on the table, and attacked his breakfast with a gusto befitting the woman who'd prepared it. She sat across from him with her own plate, like yesterday. Only this morning was different. She moved with a relaxed grace, like this domestic scene was one of a hundred they'd already shared. A soft smile toyed at her lips. Was she thinking about last night? How they'd kissed and licked and caressed every inch of each other, sometimes fucking fast and furiously and sometimes loving as tenderly as holding a delicate flower.

In truth, neither of them had slept much. But after such a night together, his connection with her was potent. He'd catalogued every mole and dimple. Every sigh and moan. The way the flush of arousal drifted across her skin like clouds across a summer sky. Damn if he wasn't getting hard again at the thought.

She looked at him over the rim of her coffee mug, a sly glint in their caramel depths. Swallowing the last bite of bacon, he canted his head. "What is it?"

A soft chuckle escaped her lips as she rose, taking their plates to the sink and returning to refill the coffee mugs. "I was, um, thinking about how much I enjoyed your exercise regimen."

Her voice was low and velvety, and shot straight to his cock. His right arm wrapped around her hips and pulled her closer. She set the pot on the table and straddled his waist without hesitation, her breath hitching when his erection nudged her entrance through his sweats. "Be careful." He growled, nudging against her neck. "Or you'll get a morning work-out, too."

She wrapped her arms around his neck and tilted her head back, a throaty, womanly laugh rolling past lips still plumped and red from last night. "Promise? What'll it be this time? Squats? Push-ups? Something to build my core strength?"

He smiled against the pulse at her neck. He couldn't remember the last time he'd enjoyed playful morning-after banter. Maybe he'd been wrong to live so cloistered from others over the years. This teasing was a light in his darkness, a beam of joy and purpose he'd been without for longer than he cared to contemplate.

Crack! Smash!

"Damn!" scalding coffee poured over his skin from where his cyborg hand had crushed the mug in its grip. The involuntary flinch of his arm had knocked the whole pot off the table and against the cabinet. Hope and joy blinked out as despair rushed in again.

With reflexes faster than his, Eve popped off his lap and covered his hand with a napkin. She tugged at him. "Move your ass, Lehman. Let's get you to the sink."

"But the coffee..." His protest was cut short when she dragged him like an errant child to the sink.

"We can make more coffee." She turned on the water, moving his arm so the cold stream hit where the hot coffee had burned. She lifted a shoulder in a shrug. "You might be getting new kitchen appliances when you redecorate."

The laughing wink she sent him did nothing to ease the ever-present worry in his chest. He was deluded to think he could have a relationship. Or happiness. Or any of the things normal, non-cybernetic humans could have. He glared at his damn hand, the skin red from its contact with coffee but otherwise fine. But he knew what lay beneath that layer of lab-grown flesh. It was why he couldn't have nice things. Why he couldn't have Eve.

"Why bother replacing it?" God his voice sounded petulant even to his own ears. "It'll just get broken, too."

She had wrapped his hand in a clean dish towel and was carefully drying it, her movements slow and thoughtful. She cleared her throat. "You know, I can fix you." Her voice was a hesitant whisper, but he heard her just fine. "I mean, I'm sure someone can fix you."

Shaking his head, Adam pulled his hand away and grabbed paper towels, squatting to gather shards of glass coffee pot and mop the cooling contents pooled on the floor. Careful to keep her bare feet out of the proof of his folly, she bent to get his attention, but he maintained his focus on the task at hand, effectively shutting her out. It was for the best. Not like she was going to stay once she'd handed over the information she carried. She would begin a new life somewhere else. Somewhere far away from a glitching old cyborg with no life and only a fool's hope of keeping anyone safe. She deserved better than him anyway. A bar bouncer. An ex-cop. A cyborg. Wasn't like she could take him to office holiday parties or introduce him to her friends. *This is my boyfriend. Oh, ignore my bruises and broken bones. Just glitch—er, accidents. He didn't mean to—*

"—fuck me again?" Eve's voice pierced his maudlin thoughts.

His head whipped toward where she stood, shirt lifted to her chin, her naked body a glorious invitation. His eye shorted out. "What?"

She dropped the shirt and leaned against the counter. "You

weren't listening to me, so I asked if you wanted to fuck again. At least I got your attention."

If only he could accept her offer. She followed him as he carried his pile of paper towels and glass to the trash. "Adam, don't shut me out. I know you think you'll hurt me or I'm not safe here, but it doesn't have to be that way." She laid a hand on his left arm and he whirled around so that side was furthest from her, his heart hammering. Didn't she realize her life was at risk around him? As if in answer, she rested her hands on his chest. "Adam, the information on how to fix you is on the mini-drive. We only need someone with the hands-on skills to make it happen. Surely we can find someone willing to do it. Trust me."

He shook his head and stepped away from the hope she offered. "This isn't an issue of a faulty electrode or internet protocol. What's wrong with me is simple. I'm a combination computer and jackhammer. Those parts were never meant to be joined, so are wearing down too fast."

He leaned forward so she could not miss the ring of truth in his words. "Man… Machine… whatever part you look at. I'm well past my warranty, darlin'. I'm dying."

Spinning, he marched back to the bedroom to take a shower, each step away from the beauty and lightness of Eve sounding like a death knell.

Chapter Twenty

Once again, Eve hoped to blend in with the crowd.

This time, she was grateful for the casual clothing Adam had insisted on buying at a thrift store near his house. As much as she loved the intimacy of wearing his T-shirts, they were a little risqué for a Monday lunch crowd, and her stylish suit would have been too conspicuous. Fortunately, her beige capri pants, slip-on sneakers, and pink tank fit right in with the laid-back mix of college students, young mothers, tourists, day-joggers, and diners milling around the north end of the Indianapolis Canal Walk, a contemporary gathering place which had long ago been a manmade water channel. The canal's water source was here, tumbling forth from the aesthetic canal gate and into a circular water basin surrounded by a terraced lawn and eateries with plentiful outdoor seating.

Strolling with as much nonchalance as she could muster, even though she was certain the pounding of her heart could be heard across town, she looked around like she was merely taking in the scenery of the lovely day and location, hoping to catch sight of Candice. Eve had proposed this time and location to meet with the newswoman, and hoped she would show. There were enough people around that meeting with someone wouldn't appear odd, and also hopefully enough people to deter any potential killer. Unlike the dark alley with MadDog, any murder attempt would have a witness. And she'd only need to scream to cause a panicked hysteria which might provide enough distraction for her to escape.

At least, that was what Adam had said about her proposed meeting location. She sent a silent *thank you* to Betty for the suggestion, as Adam had approved of it. He'd outlined a plan allowing for secret signals, multiple exit points, drilled her on what to be on the lookout for, and shown her a few basic maneuvers should anyone grab her. If she hadn't had MadDog die in her arms, she might have assumed Adam was paranoid. Of course, if MadDog hadn't died, she wouldn't be in this situation.

Which meant she wouldn't have spent last night in Adam's arms. Her nipples pearled at the memory of his attentive and inventive lovemaking, the memory only slightly dimmed by his emotional and physical retreat this morning. Knowing he was a cyborg explained the slight metallic aspect of his manly scent, and why he was so quick to retreat from physical contact. And why he insisted that being with him was hazardous to her health.

Plopping onto a limestone bench to observe the noonday flow of people around the basin, flocked with a few paddle-boaters and automaton ducks—all the cuteness with none of the poop—she adjusted her baseball cap and tightened her ponytail. Then, she dug into the bag of muffins she carried, pulling out a chocolate chip one. This had been Adam's idea, to hide the mini-drive in a muffin. If something happened, she could drop the bag, run, and return for it later. If nothing happened, she could hand it to Candice and walk away.

For someone who insisted he was a danger to her, Adam worked hard to keep her safe.

She nibbled the muffin, glancing around, comparing everybody against what Adam had coached her to observe. Like the woman across the way with a baby stroller big enough to hide a compact assault rifle. She stopped and bent, reaching toward the stroller's contents. Eve's heart flinched and she nearly dropped the muffin and ran, but the woman straightened with a baby in her arms, and proceeded to sit and pull aside her blouse to nurse.

There was the suspicious man dining outside the quaint bistro atop the small hill. He wore sunglasses and an earpiece. He was alone, staring in her direction, likely communicating her whereabouts to a rooftop sniper. Eve tensed, her mouth turned to ash, but a woman appeared at the table and greeted the man, who put his earpiece down—his phone, now that she got a better view—and stood, pulling the woman into a loving embrace.

Eve's nerves were fraught, and she'd only been at this for half an hour. How did spies do this sort of thing full-time? She was ready to jump out of her skin, and a dull tension headache throbbed at her temples.

She continued to nibble on her muffin and surreptitiously glance around, this time gazing past the jogger who rounded the curve of the pond from the opposite direction she had come. Dressed in black shorts and a steel-gray long-sleeved compression shirt, sunglasses and a ball cap, he stood out like a sore thumb against the colorful parade of people on this sunny day. Or maybe that was less due to his subdued choice in color and more the fact he was sexy as hell. Muscled and sculpted like a gladiator statue. Like a sleek wild panther. Like all her midnight fantasies come to life.

Maybe he stood out because she knew exactly how much that powerful body could rock her world.

Eve licked the muffin crumbs off her lips and mentally berated herself for acting like a horny teenager, willing the surging wave of arousal to recede. She was a middle-aged woman in a dangerous crisis. This was an inopportune time to be ruled by hormones, especially when those same hormones had never been so boisterous before.

When Adam stretched on the concrete ledge surrounding the pond, his muscles—and other body parts—popping and bulging against the body-hugging fabric, her mouth watered for more than the dry, tasteless muffin she chewed.

Maybe she was having a hot flash, because all she wanted to do was throw her clothes off and jump his bones.

Before Eve could wrangle the flare of heat consuming her body, a woman dressed more professionally than the setting called for approached to the side. Statuesque, with a showstopper smile and an intricate crown of braids, Candice Abara commanded attention, and several people glanced her direction. She stopped a few feet from the other end of the bench. "Are you the person who has something for me?"

Heart quivering in her throat, Eve lifted her gaze and pasted a starstruck expression on her face. "Candice Abara from channel twelve?"

"Yes, I am." Candice confirmed with a hesitant nod of her head. "And are you the—"

"Oh my heavens, you're even more stunning in person." Eve gushed.

Candice seemed uneasy, which was odd for an investigative reporter who no doubt was accustomed to meeting strangers and addressing sensitive topics. But she rallied and waved her hand dismissively. "You're so sweet to say that. I'm here looking for someone. Are you the person who has something for me?"

She was close enough to talk but far enough away that… That something seemed off. But Eve couldn't place what it was. Candice's odd more-than-personal-space distance? Her approach from the side rather than direct? The tension in her body? Her stiff smile, less friendly and more predatory? Damn, Adam's paranoia was rubbing off on Eve.

In her peripheral, he rose and jogged back the way he'd come.

Her cue to abort.

Eve shook her head and tried to appear confused by Candice's question. "I'm sorry, no. I have muffins, but they're for the family."

Candice frowned and her eyes darted to the side like she was checking something. "Sorry to disturb you." She muttered before turning and marching away.

Eve dropped the half-eaten muffin back into the bag, and ambled up the nearby stairs toward street level. At least, she tried to amble. But the adrenalin coursing through her body turned her retreat into more of an awkward power walk even as her brain shouted at her to look casual. Teeth clenched to keep from screaming, breath coming in gulps, thankful for the sunglasses so no one would notice the crazed back-and-forth darting of her gaze, she desperately meandered the circuitous path Adam had set for her if he decided they needed to abandon the plan. She almost missed his car as he rounded a corner and pulled up beside her.

Sliding into the passenger seat with a fluid ease she didn't feel, she closed the door and slumped to be less visible. Adam drove without a word, winding expertly through the downtown streets until the looming skyscrapers disappeared from her angled view through the windows.

"Eve, you gotta breath." His soft murmur preceded a quick but gentle squeeze of her shoulder.

She choked back a laugh which would have come out high-pitched and hysterical and wouldn't help anything.

"Keep it together, darlin'." He was talking to his car again. Except, he hadn't called his car by that particular endearment the other night. But he'd used it on Eve. In fact, he used it on her with increasing frequency. She might have mustered indignation he knew the secret to her complicity, except her heart rate slowed and her muscles relaxed, the terror of a few minutes ago evaporating from her cells.

With her world imploding and her life at stake, a few simple words from him calmed her and gave her strength. In a situation where she didn't trust anyone, she trusted Adam implicitly. With her secret, her body, and—if she was being honest—her heart. Which was particularly funny, because he didn't trust himself.

The car slowed and turned, then crunched over gravel. From her viewpoint, he hadn't taken them home. There was no garage, only trees, their leaves waving happily in welcome. He shut off the engine. "C'mon, let's stretch our legs."

Pulling her wobbly body out of the car, she took the hand he offered her and walked to a picnic table under a dense copse of trees. He'd driven to a small park in a neighborhood of stately modern homes. Cheery flowers and majestic oak trees waved and bobbed in a humid summer breeze. The August heat pressed against her skin almost painfully, contrasting so sharply with the chill which had seeped down to her bones.

Eve raised her face to the sunlight flickering through the branches, closing her eyes and breathing deep. She didn't look at Adam, but sensed him, solid and capable, seated beside her. He grumbled, a muffled curse directed at himself, and his warm lips descended in hers.

The kiss was short, but definitely sweet. Hot, in fact. She smiled as he pulled away, and opened her eyes. He looked less than happy. "Can't fucking keep my hands off you."

Even grumpy Adam couldn't erase Eve's satisfaction that he was equally as flummoxed as she by this intense attraction simmering between them. She rested her chin on his shoulder. "So what made you signal to abort? What did you see?"

He frowned, his whole demeanor darkening. "I didn't see anything specific. Just a tingle in my back. A gut instinct I've learned to listen to."

"Ooooh, gut instinct. Is that one of your Big Scary Cyborg enhancements?" It wasn't, but the temptation to tease him was irresistible, especially after he'd made such a big deal about being so damn dangerous. The glare he sent her was tinged with laughter. "Have you ever not listened to your gut?"

He nodded, staring at the ground in front of him. "Once. It's why I'm now what I am."

He couldn't admit it out loud, not that she blamed him. Years of trying to hide his cyborg parts, keeping the information away from the fickle public which could swiftly turn. He'd had to hide who he was for so long, the concealment had become second nature.

She sighed and rested her hand on his thigh. The muscle beneath flinched. After a moment's hesitation, he wrapped his right arm around her shoulders, tucking her closely. His outdated condoms proved he hadn't been intimate in a long while, and his fear he'd glitch and hurt someone likely kept him from any sort of voluntary physical contact. Adam had denied himself the touch of another, and no doubt craved it. She knew exactly what he'd given up. Since her divorce, she'd been without the physical proximity of someone who cared about her. In hindsight, she'd been without since even before the divorce.

"You know, Adam, you're not the only one who has suffered a life of solitude." She leaned further into the comfort of his embrace. "Humans are pack animals. We're not meant to be alone. We wither as surely as a plant without the sun. Maybe your self-isolation is prompting the glitches."

"So, I should go out into the world and make friends?" His tone held no derision, but he was obviously humoring her. "Or maybe look for a Cyborg's Anonymous group?"

She shrugged. "Or create one yourself. There are support groups for all kinds of at-risk individuals. Alcoholics, drug-users, injured military. Maybe by finding others dealing with the same issues, you could come to terms with your own."

"Hmmm. What would our twelve steps be? Admit you're a cyborg? Seek out your hapless victims and apologize? Call your cyborg sponsor when you feel like you're going to rampage a city?"

She swatted his arm, laughing. "You forgot to include *forgive yourself.*" She pulled away so she could reposition to straddle his lap and look him straight in the eye. "Okay, so maybe the support group doesn't resemble any others. But wouldn't it would be nice to have a safe place to go and share your concerns? Support each other? Have someone you know you can depend on?"

Eve ran her hands up and down his arms, from broad shoulders to where his large hands gripped her hips. Correction, his *right* hand gripped. The left hand was a fist, gripping only itself. She frowned, her heart weeping at what he'd surely experienced over the years, with no one to tell him he mattered or they cared whether he lived or died. "Wouldn't you like to have someone to share your life with, to live for? Someone who loves you? Someone you can love in return?"

As soon as the questions were out of her mouth, she cringed. They sounded like she was trying to get him to admit he loved her. While such a declaration might be nice, she didn't expect it. His expression hardened, his jaw muscles bulging. "If you're trying to tug at my heartstrings, they don't exist. And you know as well as I do that living with me is dangerous to anyone's health."

She might not have expected him to claim he loved her, but his answer disappointed nonetheless. "That's not what I'm getting at, dammit. I'm saying maybe you should try living again, not just existing in this purgatory you've kept yourself in all these years, bound by fear and worry."

One eyebrow lifted in disbelief. She crossed her arms over her chest and glowered at him. "I'm not saying go make a cyborg-coming-out parade float. If you were trying to live instead of waiting to die, you might find things aren't as bad as you think."

"Okay Pollyanna-with-the-proof-someone's-out-to-kill-me." He stood, holding her until she could get her feet under her. "Let's say I start a support group and build a network of fellow cyborgs who provide emotional encouragement for each other. How does that keep *you* safe?"

She waved her arms, with no real answer for him. "It doesn't. But this isn't about me. I'll have given my information to someone and you won't have to worry about some sniper trying to kill me."

He placed his hands on her shoulders, frowning. "I'm not talking about the attempts on your life. How will it keep you safe from me? We've been damn lucky so far. I've only destroyed some furniture. Next time—"

"Adam, trust yourself because I do. You won't hurt me." Not entirely true. She was certainly at risk of getting her heart broken. But that wasn't what he feared, and he was already shaking his head to deny her statement.

"You keep saying that, but—" His eyebrows shot up, his hands clenching her arms. A heartbeat later, he shoved her toward the ground. "Under the table. Drone."

Her heart in her throat, her gut at her feet, Eve scrambled under the table as Adam ripped off the molded resin seat bolted to the metal frame and hunkered down with her, using the board as a shield. Eve tried to listen for the whirring sound of the drone, but only heard the thundering pulse of her heart and the harsh passage of air through her mouth. A glance to her right proved Adam was as calm as a cucumber, like he dealt with this sort of terror every day.

As a cyborg trying to keep his glitching body hidden from public scrutiny, maybe he did.

"You know, being with me is hazardous to your health." Eve muttered under her breath, tossing his own words back at him. A poorly-timed jest, but he chuckled anyway.

Adam lowered the board so he could look as far into the sky

as the table top would allow. His gaze tracked something, his cyborg eye nearly glowing with intensity. He lifted the board as she heard a quiet *pew pew,* then something hit the board with a resounding *tink-tink.*

"Those aren't bullets." He growled. "It's shooting darts. Probably the same kind that got MadDog."

They were at risk of dying in that same horrible manner? She bit back the scream tearing through her throat. A high-pitched buzzing approached, weaving back and forth like a swarm of angry hornets. If only they were dealing with such a benign enemy as stinging insects. Adam whipped the board in his hands like a bat and swung at the drone. He cursed as the buzzing zoomed backward out of reach. It whizzed over toward the other side of the table.

"Tilt it!" He hefted the table onto its side as he gave the order. Eve held onto the side supports to keep the table from tumbling forward onto its top and leaving them exposed.

The dance ensued for what seemed like hours, but was probably only a couple minutes. Adam swung the board without making contact, the buzzing zipped around, the *pew* continued to pellet them, *tinking* against the table and board. They tilted and rotated their meager barricade until her arms threatened to fall off.

A *pew* hit the ground near where Eve kneeled and she yelped, staring at the tiny death dart which looked like part of a child's miniature toy set.

"This is futile. We need a diversion." Adam growled beside her. He might have cybernetic implants, but he was still a man. How much longer could he keep up?

"Would it track my hat if I threw it?" She raked her baseball cap off her head. "Which direction do you want it?"

He jerked his head toward her right and nodded. She tossed her projectile into the air. At the same time, he stood and hefted the board, throwing it like a spear. It hit the drone, which lurched sideways, its broken propellers dragging it downward. Adam had already leaped over the table and lifted the board again, swatting at the drone, smashing it against a nearby tree trunk. The whirring buzz staggered to a halt, its absence ringing in Eve's ears.

Her flood of relief flushed away as soon as Adam turned. A dart, no bigger than her fingernail, dangled from his shirt, above his heart. He'd been shot, no doubt with the virus which had killed MadDog. Images of Adam, mouth foaming and eyes bleeding, gurgling his last breath in her arms, flashed through her head and her legs gave out. She tumbled to the ground, her insides hollow and her head wailing. Or maybe that was her throat. She'd rather be dead than have Adam suffer so.

"Eve, darlin', what's wrong?" His worried voice was nearby, warm hands on her arms, lifting her against a hard wall of muscled heat.

"Y-you were hit. In the chest." She sniffed, swallowing back her sobs enough to tell him what was in her heart before he died. "Oh, God Adam! I'm so sorry! You're the most amazing man I've ever met, and I love you and I hate that you're going to die when you were only trying to protect me from the drone and… and… why are you smiling?"

Was this a side effect of the virus? Or perhaps a different strain? Adam looked unconcerned he was about to bleed his insides out through all his orifices. "Eve, I wasn't hit. It snagged on the shirt but didn't get me. I'm not going to die on you." He grimaced and flicked the miniscule dart off his shirt. "At least not from the virus."

"So…" She blinked, willing her brain to kick back into gear so she could process what he'd said and her own verbal spewing.

"So, we're both alive and unscathed." He finished for her. "You gonna take back what you said about loving me?"

Her gut clenched at the thought, as much as it had when they'd been under attack. She drew a deep breath and shook her head. "No. After everything we've been through, I would be insincere to pretend I'm not in love with you or claim you're not the most amazing man I've ever met."

He didn't return her sentiments, but neither did he make any pathetic excuses for why he didn't or couldn't love her. Instead, he kissed her, his tongue swiping her lips like a promise before he pulled back. "We need to get away from here and under cover before they send more drones."

Eve nodded and followed him back to the car. Her emotions were jumbled and chaotic, a haphazard soup of adrenalin rush, constant fear for her life, unrequited love, and a healthy dose of desire for the sexy man beside her. Her muscles were lead weights, and the thought of having to defend against another attack brought tears to her eyes. How could they continue like this? The odds were stacked against them with no hope in sight. And if Adam decided she was too much trouble and left her to fend for herself, she wouldn't last a minute. In truth, the only reason she was still alive was thanks to him.

He drove the car with a steady hand, his face a mask of intense focus. Selfless, thoughtful, always putting her needs and safety ahead of his own. If she could design the perfect man, she wouldn't change an inch of him. She didn't regret loving him. Even if he didn't love her in return.

Chapter Twenty-One

A dam's brain worked overtime as he drove them home, but not on anything that would help them in their current situation. As if his processor was stuck on a loading screen, it circled endlessly around three words. *I love you.* Eve had uttered them, then reaffirmed them. And he hadn't said a thing.

He glanced down where she dozed against his shoulder. He didn't blame her for sleeping. His own muscles grew increasingly lethargic from last night's lack of sleep, the night and day's physical expenditure, and the expected post-adrenaline low from their attack. The rusty, clanking gears of his brain were the only thing keeping him awake at the wheel, grinding over and over again that powerful statement. *I love you.*

Why? What did she see in him, a washed-up cop, a dumb bar bouncer, a broken cyborg. She thought he was amazing. She accepted him, cybernetic parts and all, without hesitation. She desired him, knowing exactly what he was, when the rest of the world would squawk at the insult of breathing the same air. She trusted him. Depended on him. Wanted to help him, fix him.

She aspired to make a world where he and other cyborgs could walk in the open without shame or fear.

He loved her, but not for these reasons. They merely reaffirmed his feelings, the listing of each fact followed by a *Yes of course, because the woman I love would be this.* As if his heart had always known. Or perhaps the progression of that emotion had been a subtle progression he'd been too distracted to notice. All this time, he'd assumed the thumping mechanical gearbox in his chest left him incapable of such tender emotions.

Whatever the case, did he dare trust this feeling? Maybe it was heartburn. Or another glitch, one potentially more dangerous to his own well-being than a flexing arm.

Do you trust me, Adam?

Dr. Farrow's calming words turned in his head.

Yeah, Doc. I trust you. I just don't trust myself.

He'd trusted Doc. And he trusted Eve. If she loved him, that would be enough.

He pulled into his garage and turned the car off, the sudden end to the rumbling motor like a switch turning off his questions and doubts. He loved this woman. The tingle in his spine, and the warmth which infused him with the realization… was this what *happiness* felt like? After so many damn years alone, he barely recognized the emotion. His lips curved upward of their own volition. He loved Eve. With every cell and synthetic fiber of his being. A truly odd epiphany for a man who had assumed his cybernetic heart couldn't feel that tender emotion. But there it was, as true as the North Star, and hopefully as legendary of a guide for a sailor in uncharted waters such as he.

"Darlin', wake up." Adam murmured against Eve's temple.

He bent his head to her hair and inhaled her floral scent. He could drink her in all day. What he wouldn't give to carry her straight to his bedroom so he could show her exactly how much he loved her although he hadn't said the words—they'd gotten stuck in his throat at the park—then fall into a peaceful sleep in her arms. If only they had time on their side, but they didn't.

The tranquil darkness of his garage gave the impression such a thing was possible. But it was a lie. Death was headed their way. The question was what form would it take?

And how much time did they have to prepare.

Eve stirred, stretching, then jerked awake, tense and alert. "Shhh, it's okay, darlin'. We're home." Her head swiveled to his, the terror in her eyes vanishing as soon as she focused on him. She trusted him to keep her safe, like how he'd once been entrusted as an officer to keep the public safe. Like how he'd trusted Doc. For some reason, none of that filled him with the joy of knowing this beautiful, capable woman believed in him unconditionally.

Adam had never prayed before, but he did now. Prayed he'd be worthy of Eve. Prayed he could keep her safe. Prayed that at the end of this, he might have the chance and the courage to tell her how much he loved her.

Prayed she'd understand if he didn't.

She placed a hand on his thigh and smiled, the picture so reminiscent of last night's lovemaking, desire skittered along his spine. "So what's the plan?"

He clamped down on his igniting arousal and cleared his throat. "All I've got so far is *stay alive.*"

The hand on his thigh lifted to cup his cheek. "You're funny." She leaned over and kissed him.

Arousal broke free and shot straight to his groin. He deepened the kiss, pouring his heart into it, hoping she would hear the words he couldn't speak. He pulled back just far enough for a confession—"I really don't have a plan..."—before she pulled him back to her welcoming lips. Their tongues twined, their breaths mingled, their soft sighs rang out.

She reached out and pulled his hand—his left hand—to cup her breast. The woman trusted him more than he trusted himself, and images of his mattress popped into his brain. Rather than risk his cyborg hand glitching and squeezing her breast to a pulp, he pulled back and rubbed the knuckles around and across the puckered nipple. She moaned into his mouth and arched, an invitation to take that delicious morsel of a breast into his mouth, and damn if he didn't want that more than he wanted his next breath.

She pulled away, a devious smile on her plumped lips. "You know, we could take this to the bedroom."

He rested his forehead against hers, panting and willing his dick to stop clamoring for attention. Their lives were in danger, remember? "We shouldn't. Not now. We need to gather supplies and get ready for a quick getaway."

"You think they'll find us here?" She frowned.

How much to admit without scaring her? "I think we shouldn't assume they won't."

She nodded, taking that bit of information in stride. "If we need to prepare for a quick getaway, why are we still in the car?"

"Some of my scanners are glitching. I need to brute force them back online."

She pulled back, her gaze roving his face like a caress, and smiled. Open, trusting, content. "Okay. While you brute force yourself, I have to go to the bathroom."

She grabbed his key out of the ignition and slid out of the car. The backdoor opened without the keys. She screwed her face in laughter at the unnecessary effort to claim them, and trotted through the house door. He bashed his head against the side window to shake his systems back. His gut churned from something... something amiss... there was something wrong, his Spidey-senses screamed. His heat signature vision flickered back online, and he knew what was wrong as soon as he saw the latent handprint on the open door. The handprint too large to be Eve's.

He'd locked the door when they'd left.

His gut dropped at the same time Eve screamed.

Adam dashed into the house with lightning speed, heaving to a stop at the end of the hall, his arms braced against the walls, ready to launch at whatever was attacking Eve.

She stood in the middle of the open area between kitchen and living room, her hand on her heart, laughing.

"…me a heart attack, I didn't see you standing there. Are you a friend of Adam's?"

Confusion tumbled through him. He had no friends. Was Eve in danger? She didn't act like she was in trouble. She turned to him. "Adam, you didn't tell me you were expecting a friend. I would have made a crudité plate." A stranger might assume she was lightly admonishing him for a social slight, but he saw her fear. Worry pulled at her expression, tension forced her voice higher and more brittle.

For whatever reason, she was playing like this was nothing out of the ordinary. He forced down the urge to maim and kill, sauntered up to her, and slung his arm around her waist, kissing her on the temple. Was this how couples behaved? He barely remembered. "I didn't want to worry you, honey."

Prepared to shove her out of danger's way, he looked in the direction she spoke. A man stood in the middle of his living room as if he'd been invited, yet he fairly vibrated with uncertainty. Adam's officer training kicked into gear as he quickly took in the man's stats. Early forties. Five-eight. Close-cropped black hair with a brush of silver at his temple. Physique beefy, a once-fit body suffering from middle age spread. Jeans and a simple black tee showed no signs of hidden weapons, though he was likely armed. Something about the face pinged Adam's memory bank. He'd seen this man in the news years ago. He'd been grieved. He'd been…

A firefighter. Injured when a house collapsed on him. The hint of burn scars crept up his neck. He'd been pronounced dead, but here he was. Which meant…

Cyborg.

All his systems on high alert, his brain racing for possible scenarios and how to keep Eve safe in each of them, Adam forced his lips to turn upward in a semblance of a smile. "David

Sanchez. I remember reading about you in the papers. Welcome to our home."

Eve turned, pulling from his arms, and kissed him on the cheek. She turned to David. "A pleasure to meet you, David. Can I get you something to drink? Coffee, maybe, or are you ready for a beer?" She called the last over her shoulder as she walked to the kitchen.

She knew. Knew there was a cyborg intruder standing right there, likely with orders to kill her. Yet she acted like nothing was amiss. And for his part, David looked confused, like he wasn't sure why he was here. "Wh-who are you?"

"Adam Lehmann. Former IMPD."

"Okay. But why am I in your home?"

Adam shrugged. "That was my next question. You don't know?"

"I remember walking here and opening your front door." David frowned as if his memories made no sense. Adam frowned because someone had jimmied his locks. "But why would I come here?"

Maybe David wasn't under orders. Or maybe his orders were of a more subliminal nature. Maybe they were—

Downloaded.

Damn, that was the key, wasn't it? Cyborgs had a modem so they could receive system updates, receive bulletins like APBs and Amber Alerts, and access the internet for searches on criminal databases. What if those system updates were of a more sinister nature? Like the cyborg in Chicago, destroying cars even as he seemed to fight against his own actions. He'd been acting against his will, possibly trying to refuse the irrefutable commands given to his cybernetic parts.

If someone could command a cyborg to kill against his will, what else could they do? Command the heart to stop beating? Command the lungs to seize. Command the brain to turn on loved ones? Was this what Eve was fighting to prevent? If so, her mission and her information were more important than merely saving some beat-up first-responders. It was life and death for all cyborgs. And more.

"I don't know why you're here, David." Adam admitted. Letting David stay meant keeping Eve in danger. But this might be their only chance to get some answers. "So until we figure that out, let's assume it's a friendly visit."

Adam could be amicable with a fellow cyborg, and still keep his guard.

Eve entered the room, three bottles in her hands. "You didn't specify, so I figured what's a beer between friends? Please have a seat, David." She handed him a beer, gave one to Adam, and took a sip of her own.

Like they entertained all the time. Like any of this was normal. And wasn't that brilliant on her part? Reach out to the human part of David, remind him he was so much more than his cybernetics. Just like she'd shown Adam he was more than a broken, malfunctioning appliance.

"Make yourself at home." Adam motioned toward the couch and moved to a chair facing it. "Sorry for the mess, but we're starting some home renovations."

The words came out as natural as truth, as if he and Eve had been together, their lives aligned, for years. Was this how a relationship should be? Even with the underlying threat of this other cyborg going rogue, it felt good. Natural.

David sat, beer in hand, expression almost comical in his confusion. Too bad none of this was funny.

Eve sat her luscious backside on the edge of the footstool, her legs stretched out and ankles crossed. She reached forward and clinked her bottle against David's before sitting back and taking another drink. "So, David. Tell me about yourself."

Adam took a drink as well. "I remember the report about your accident years back. I'm no firefighter, but that looked like a helluva fire. Then to have it collapse on you… Man, glad you've healed from it."

David nodded, brows furrowed as if not quite sure what to say, or why they were having this crazy-civil conversation. "Yeah, I, uh… it took a while… still got scars… but I was offered some experimental services—"

He stopped, no doubt afraid to admit he'd signed the cybernetic contract. Adam understood his hesitation. It wasn't something you readily admitted to anyone. Eve leaned forward, her voice soft with understanding. "David, did they implant you with cybernetic systems? Adam has them, too, and I'm so grateful because it means he's still alive." She reached over and caressed his arm, the love in her eyes taking his breath away. "Giving good men and women a second chance is why the cybernetic program was created."

"Not everyone is as accepting as you." David grumbled, and Adam heard the echo of his own bitterness. "They think we're going to lose control of our parts and"—his brows furrowed on the thought—"hurt people."

Eve waved the concern away with a laugh. "Hollywood sure has a distorted view of the world, doesn't it? If I believed everything I've seen in the movies and on TV, zombies and quicksand would be a much bigger problem than they are."

Adam snickered at the truth. Beer to his lips, he interjected. "Don't forget alien invasions and clowns."

"Yes!" She laughed. "Ghosts. Intergalactic battles between superheroes and super-villains. Weather-related shark attacks…"

As Eve listed the outrageous threats Hollywood had depicted, David smiled and chuckled as well. He relaxed enough to take a drink of his beer.

Eve tucked her legs and leaned forward, her expression one of determination. "David, your cybernetic systems aren't *parts,* separate from the man you are. They're not chicken nuggets. You are all of this." She waved to indicate his entire body, and Adam knew she was speaking to him as much as she was David. "A kidney transplant patient fully integrates the organ so the body becomes one again. Your body has integrated your cybernetic systems so you are David, the human being. Not David, the half-guy-half-robot thing."

David shook his head. "But the half-robot in me glitches. I can't always control it."

She speared him with a look. "I can't always control my body. If I could, I'd never stub my toes on furniture or snore or miss my mouth when I eat."

He smiled and took another sip of beer, looking sheepishly at the carpet. "Yeah, I guess you have a point."

She did, although Adam hesitated to point out her non-cyborg "glitches" didn't destroy furniture or shred mattresses or threaten lives. Guess the benefit of greater strength came with the downside of greater snafus. Like having an elephant step on your foot versus a dog, the act would be more painful due to the weight, not because an elephant is a more vicious creature.

Speaking of elephants, the metaphorical one in the room sat quietly on the couch, nodding and contemplating Eve's words. Maybe she'd gotten through to him. Maybe he wasn't a threat to her life. Maybe this would turn out alright.

Adam was about to relax in his chair when his lower back tingled.

And David lunged for Eve.

Chapter Twenty-Two

E ve could only flinch as David hurtled toward her. Adam
broadsided him, and they veered to the right, crashing to
the ground. She wasn't about to jump in the fray, so she darted
out of arm's reach, jumping over the couch and stumbling when
her back foot caught on the way over—Dammit, if only she were
in her twenties again—and she ran to the kitchen. Her heart
cringed and her lungs seized, her hands trembling more than they
had at the park, as she yanked open drawers to search for something, anything, she could use to stop the fight.

She winced at the harsh sounds of bottles smashing and
punches landing on flesh. Two cyborgs fought in the other room,
one trying to kill her and the other trying to defend her. And she
wanted both to live. Killing one cyborg to save another made no
sense. Neither did killing a cyborg to protect the information she
carried about Preditech killing cyborgs.

She grabbed a large chef's knife from a drawer. Then put it
back. She was just as likely to cut Adam or herself, and anything
she did to incapacitate David might also make him bleed out.
She grabbed the toaster. Maybe she could hurl it and conk him
on the head. She dropped it back on the counter. A rolling pin

would be a better weapon for conking. But did Adam even own one?

A loud crash jerked her attention to the living room. Two powerful bodies grappled, pitched, and rolled over the top of the couch, upending it as they landed with a thud which shook the house. They wrestled, the mass of their two bodies swaying and teetering. There was no way she could place a hit without getting both and maybe getting caught in their wake. On a squeal, she jumped on the counter, yanking her legs out of the way as the entangled mass crashed against the cabinets where she'd stood a moment ago.

Adam was bigger and David wasn't as muscular, but he didn't go down easily. As they hurled against the kitchen table, which crumpled beneath their weight. Eve spotted blood. It left a trail as they wrestled, trying to bite and rip and squeeze the life out of each other.

Flaps of flesh dangled, the metal and translucent cables of cybernetic parts were visible like an exposed computer. Power-chips, data cords, expansion busses. If she could stick something there, a fork or knife maybe, she might be able to short out David's system. But again, they were a blur of movement and she was a horrid shot.

Desperate to help, she looked around the kitchen again, her eyes catching the faucet sprayer attachment. Yes! Water would short out circuitry better than any utensils, and she wouldn't have to get close. She grabbed the nozzle and aimed, waiting for a clear shot. The bodies convulsed again, rolling, before pausing with David's exposed back to her. She let loose the stream of water.

David seized, gasping and convulsing, his head thrown back, then went limp in Adam's grip. Adam maintained his choke grip for a few heartbeats before realizing the other cyborg no longer fought back. He reluctantly released the neck and unfurled from the tangle of arms and legs, panting, his expression confused and uncertain. He looked from David to Eve and back. "You did that?"

"Yes, I did." She let the nozzle drop into the sink and hopped off the counter and raced over to pat him down, worried about his injuries. "Are you okay? Where are you hurt? Are you bleeding? We need to get you to a doctor—"

Adam pulled her against his chest and held her. "I'm ok, just bruised from a few lucky hits. David got the worst of it. I bounce angry drunks for a living, remember."

Weak with the relief he wasn't hurt, Eve relaxed against the warmth of his body. "I was so afraid for you. And for David."

"You were afraid for David? News flash, he was going to kill you."

"Did you see the sudden change in him before he attacked? Something happened. A glitch or something." She pulled away and framed his face in her hands. "What if this had been you? I'd want someone to avoid killing you. We can't save cyborgs if we kill them all in the attempt."

Adam shook his head and huffed out a laugh. He kissed her. "You're too compassionate. And you're right." He touched his forehead to hers before looking at David lying on the kitchen floor, the slight rise and fall of his chest a sign he was still alive. "The water shorted him out. But he'll be back online at some point. We need to get him to someone who can help him."

Eve laughed bitterly. "Yeah, but who could that be? The world seems to be decidedly against helping cyborgs."

He ran his fingers through his hair, his expression contemplative. After a moment, he nodded as if he'd made a decision. "Yeah, I know someone. My old doctor, assuming the number I have for him is still in service. We'll have to tie David up so he won't hurt anyone or himself in the meantime."

She patted Adam on the back and turned away, sidestepping David's prone form and flashing Adam a cheeky smile. "Great idea, you do that. I still have to pee."

Chapter Twenty-Three

dam was hearing things. "What?"

"I said, are you sure you don't want to go back for your *Playboys*?" Eve sat in the passenger seat, nibbling on a slightly-crushed muffin from the morning like it was an everyday occurrence to ride in a car with an unconscious cyborg hog-tied and duct-taped in the back seat and a trunk of hastily packed go-bags in case they had to leave town and maybe never return.

"Why would I want my Playboys?" There was nothing within those withered pages to compare to the flesh-and-blood woman next to him.

"You know… in case you want something to read." She shot him a confused glance, like she didn't understand why he couldn't understand her simple question.

"So, I should have my *Playboys* in case I want to read something?"

"Yeah. I understand gentlemen's publications were popular for their written articles. I looked in your third drawer that first night, even though you told me not to. But didn't have time to do much more than skim past the pictures."

Three days ago, this would have been a bizarre conversation.

Adam shook his head as he pulled off the highway. "I'm okay without my *Playboys*."

She shrugged and looked out the window with a sigh. "Fine. I just don't want you to get bored."

He snatched her hand and brought the knuckles to his lips for a kiss, unable to suppress the chuckle. "Trust me, darlin'. There's never a dull moment with you."

He wound his way along the patchy streets of the upper west side of the Indy inner loop. At the turn of the previous century, the area had been a busy industrial park with distribution warehouses spanning acres. These days, the Park 100 area was mostly abandoned and neglected, possibly boasting a significant homeless population. This was not where he would have expected Dr. Farrow to send them, but these were the directions the doc had given him. Could be he was leading them to a trap. It had been nearly seven years since Adam had last seen the physician who had helped him rehabilitate after his fateful surgery. Dr. Farrow had been patient and encouraging those first years when Adam had struggled with debilitating physical and emotional pain. The doc hadn't given up on Adam, even when he'd lashed out at the man, and neither had he allowed Adam to give up on himself.

By the third year after his surgery, Adam had overcome all the physical obstacles of integrating cybernetic systems with organic. He'd gotten his bouncer job, and had believed he'd come to terms with the abandonment of his fiancée and the entire police force. He'd determined he didn't need the good doc's rehabilitation anymore and had told him as much.

Dr. Farrow had written his personal phone number on Adam's palm. "For if you ever need me" Farrow had declared with the same enigmatic Buddha smile he always wore. Adam had stored the number in his memory even though he hadn't believed he would call the good doctor.

Hopefully Farrow meant what he'd said back then.

As the cryptic directions instructed, Adam turned the car into the receiving area of a warehouse which didn't look quite as run-down as its neighbors. A faded hand-made sign declaring this was the location for HYDROFOODS, INC. greeted them. He pulled up to dock 9, again as instructed, and flashed his high beams twice. It was still early evening and there was plenty of sunlight to drown out the headlights, so those particular instructions were pointless, but who—

The car shuddered and lowered, as if on a large elevator platform. Adam was torn between the urge to get Eve the hell away from here and curiosity over this strange twist of events. About fifteen feet down, the view out the front window opened from concrete wall to underground parking garage. A robust figure in a long white lab coat and a spray of white hair on his head waved them forward. An older Dr. Farrow than Adam remembered, but that was to be expected. They hadn't seen each other for several years.

He drove past the massive concrete pillar supports to the space the doc indicated about fifty feet from the platform lift. The lift which was raising, cutting off the evening's sunlight and their only escape. Turning the car off, he motioned to Eve to sit tight, and unwound from his seat to a stand as the doc approached.

"You've gotten old, Doc." Adam teased as he tapped his door with a hip to close it.

Farrow patted his tuft of white hair and adjusted his rimless glasses. "What can I say? It's not the years, it's the mileage."

Adam took the doctor's outstretched hand in a firm grip. Farrow laughed and thumped him on the arm, nodding toward the car. "I see you're still driving this clunker."

Holding his hand to his heart, Adam gasped in mock affront. "Clunker? This beauty is a classic."

Farrow laughed again, his gut bouncing like a jolly old elf. "Aren't we all, Adam. Aren't we all."

Adam jerked his head to indicate their surroundings. "So,

what's with the cloak-and-dagger stuff, Doc. This your Bat Cave or something?"

The inscrutable smile Farrow was known for spread across his face. His voice grew serious. "Every super hero needs a secret lair. You know that."

The passenger door creaked open and Eve popped up to look at Farrow from across the car's roof. "Hi. I'm Eve."

Farrow's smile softened and his eyes glittered with appreciation. "Greetings, my dear. I'm Dr. Timothy Farrow. Are you the reason my old patient had finally decided to call me?"

She shook her head and pointed to the back seat. "No. He is."

Farrow leaned to inspect the bound cyborg, still unconscious. The doc appeared to take such a sight in stride. Interesting. What was he accustomed to which made this situation no big deal?

"Eve, dear, could you please wheel the gurney over here?" He pointed to where the rolling cart rested against the wall as if he'd anticipated the reason for Adam's visit. "Adam, I'll let you do the heavy lifting, since I'm so old and decrepit."

He winked at Adam, who rolled his eyes in return. By the time Eve rolled the stretcher to the car, Adam had tugged David from the back seat and hefted him onto the rolling cart. Farrow leaned closer to inspect, grazing David's cheek with the back of his fingers and running a palm down his forearm.

"Hmmm. David Sanchez. Another Alpha-phase cyborg I helped rehabilitate and haven't seen in years." His voice held a wistful note. Then he cleared his throat and stood, looking over the top of his glasses at Adam. "Best to follow me in and then you can explain what happened."

With that, he marched back to where he'd parked the rolling bed, pressing his palm to a concrete block on the wall, which depressed to reveal a keypad. Farrow punched several keys and stood back. A soft whir and snick of an automated sliding door sounded as the concrete next to him shimmered and disappeared. A holographic wall that looked every bit like the actual wall beside it, covering a door. Adam shook his head. Maybe all those years of struggling to simply maintain his life and adhering to old-school, *classic* technology hadn't been the best idea. In ten short years, the world had left him behind, which was saying something for a person with advanced body parts.

They stepped through the doorway and into a brightly lit hi-tech combination laboratory-hospital. Tubes, scopes, scanners, holographic screens, robotic arms, a few examination tables, meters of counter space, and a wall of drawers spilling over with what looked like cybernetic materials.

Oh. So, less a hospital and more a pristine repair shop.

Adam's whistled low. "Helluva secret lair ya got here."

"It's been many years in the making, and I'll happily tell you about it later." A thick metal door slid closed behind them with the barest whisper. Farrow pointed to a spot for them to park the gurney. He handed Adam a pair of trauma shears. "Idle hands and all that. Now, talk to me."

Eve interjected. "Dr. Farrow, shouldn't we strap David down? He went rogue, and I'd hate for him to damage your equipment when he comes to."

Farrow was already leaning to inspect David's neck, carefully pulling off the bandage they'd hastily slapped over his wound and poking gently with a gloved hand. "It is a myth that cybernetically enhanced individuals go *rogue*, my dear. What you might consider this so-called state is merely an unfortunate override of their command center. Not unlike when you get the hiccups."

"Hiccups don't tear-ass through my house and try to kill my girlfriend." Adam muttered through clenched his teeth as he carefully pulled a length of duct tape off David's ankles.

"Oh, my. Bravo, dear Eve." Farrow's tone sounded impressed, as if Eve had worked a miracle. "You got our Adam to do the one thing I was never able to. You got him to care again."

Adam opened his mouth to argue. He cared. Dammit, he'd cared so much, he'd become a cop—until that had been snatched from him, like having his heart ripped out of his chest. He closed his mouth without uttering a word. Farrow was right. Adam had stopped caring because it hurt too much to care for a world that no longer cared about him. No, that wasn't true. He hadn't stopped caring and loving. But he had turned away from the good doctor committed to help him, and had buried those emotions deep beneath his cyborg wiring, hoping the part of him that was machine would take over and crush his feelings so he didn't have to hurt anymore.

But Eve didn't let him hide behind his synthetics. Didn't let him continue to believe he was little more than an unfeeling machine. She had proved the world wasn't entirely indifferent. She'd brought him back to Doc. She had jump-started his rusty, derelict heart, filling it with the warmth and awe of her love.

Because of her, he cared again. He was able to love again.

Only he'd never loved this deeply before.

"I didn't do anything of the sort, Doc." Eve waved off Farrow's comment. "It's the police officer in him."

And she didn't know he loved her.

Before Adam could speak, Farrow turned to him. "So, what brought you here, Adam?"

Doc didn't want details about his unspoken love for Eve or the fight with David. Adam glanced at Eve, giving her the chance to signal for silence. When she dipped her head in the barest nod, he dropped the last of the bindings and handed Farrow the shears.

"Eve worked for Preditech until a few days ago." Doc knew what Preditech was, so Adam didn't need to explain the importance of that connection. When Doc merely nodded as he continued to work on David, Adam filled him in on the rest of the story, leaving out the more intimate details of his relationship with Eve. The observant doc had likely figured that part out already.

By the end of Adam's summary of events, Farrow had dried the water out the cybernetic component at the base of David's neck. He plucked out a small chip and attached a diagnostic scanner. After a few minutes of reviewing and tweaking code, he grunted his assent, reconnected a few wires, and lowered the flap of skin. It reminded Adam of the times he turned the wrench doing routine maintenance under his car's hood. Doc sutured the wound Adam had created when he'd bit David during their tussle. The tissue would likely scar, but that couldn't be helped. Hopefully, David would forgive him in time.

As if summoned, David's eyes blinked open. He took in the scene from where he lay, his eyes filled with confusion and fear.

"Hi David. It's Dr. Farrow." Doc patted him on the shoulder and squeezed, his voice softer than when he addressed Adam. "It's good to see you again, son. Stay still. I still have some injuries to repair."

David swallowed, his eyes darting around the room. "Hi Doc. Adam. Eve. You might want to get far away from me in case I attack again."

"What makes you think you're going to attack again?" Adam asked, his teeth clenched. He stepped between Eve and the possible threat of David going rogue again. Doc might believe *rogue* was a harmless state, but Adam knew better.

"I'm so sorry." David looked past Adam to address Eve. "I don't know what happened. One minute we're talking like we've been friends for a long time, then everything went red. I remember trying to kill you, fighting Adam, and a bright flash before the darkness. And now I'm here. I didn't hurt you, either of you, did I?"

"Scared us, that's all." Eve offered.

Adam objected. "Uh, I have some nasty bruises, thank you very much."

Eve stepped to his side, her hands on her hips, and rolled her eyes. "If I promise to kiss your boo-boos, will you lighten up on David?"

Adam crossed his arm, the possibility of Eve kissing anything on his body too delicious to deny, even at the risk of sporting wood in front of David and the doc. "You'll find those boo-boos are in some... interesting... places."

Arousal lit her eyes. "Then I'll have to take extra care to kiss them properly."

"Lord, save us from horny cyborgs." Farrow muttered under his breath.

"I have to agree, Doc." David's face twisted in mock disgust. "Could you please do a memory wipe on me?"

Farrow chuckled as he finished the final stitch to the gash in David's forearm. He swiped off his surgical gloves. Motioning for David to sit, he patted him on the shoulder on the way to toss the latex wad in a trash can. "David, my boy, do you have a life you need to get back to?"

All humor left David's face, leaving him with an expression like he'd swallowed sour milk. "No. The guys at the station kept looking at me sideways after... you know... So I left. Got a bull-shit job at a garden center watering plants and hauling bags of topsoil." He sighed like a man who had no ray of sunshine in his life. Adam knew that feeling. He'd been living it, until a certain beautiful woman had walked into his bar. "Maybe they were right to worry. After all, I guess I did go rogue today, didn't I?"

"We'll have to agree to disagree on the semantics." Farrow wrapped an arm around David's shoulders and helped him to stand, before addressing the three of them. "Grab the bags I assume you brought. We'll go down to the living area. I have some information to pass along and a proposition for all of you."

Chapter Twenty-Four

Eve held Adam's hand for support as they followed Dr. Farrow, his arm still around David's shoulders as if afraid he might slip and fall. They continued down three flights of concrete stairs, deeper into the earth. Fortunately, she wasn't claustrophobic. Also fortunately, everything about the facility so far had been expansive.

Still, she was unnerved at the prospect of being so far underground, with a man who had tried to kill her and a doctor so versed in cybernetics he could just as easily be a villain if Hollywood had anything to say about it. She turned to Adam and mouthed *Do you trust him?*

He nodded. But his brows drew together, as if contemplating the possibility he *shouldn't* trust Dr. Farrow. Eve's fears were only marginally alleviated by Adam's response.

She cleared her throat. "Dr. Farrow, this facility is enormous. Do you live here?"

He chuckled. "It often seems like I do, my dear. But no, I have a small house in the Zionsville suburb. Have to keep up appearances." He waved to indicate the whole facility. "This was actually a quarantine shelter dug out by one of my great-great-

great-grandfathers in reaction to a viral outbreak in the early twenty-first century. He was a skilled engineer and a world-class prepper, according to family lore. This place is large enough to comfortably house about twenty. Fully self-contained water and air filtration systems. Natural sunlight simulation, which we use in a modified form for our HydroFoods front company at the ground-level warehouse. And I believe the supply of toilet paper might be part of the original stash he hoarded."

The stairs ended at a short corridor with a bank vault of a doorway. Another palm scan and keypad like the entry to the lab, and the door unsealed with a loud hiss of air. Dr. Farrow leaned toward them as if sharing a secret. "I've made a few upgrades over the years."

He pushed the door open and ushered them inside.

Like it had the vacuum-sealed door, air whooshed from Eve's lungs. A garden of Eden stood before them. Flowering and leafy plants in pots and hanging trellises and hydroponic towers crafted a lush jungle of vegetation around minimalist furniture in calm, watery colors. The ceiling was a domed screen of the sky, the sun edging toward the horizon at their end of the expansive room.

"I'd say your forefather was more than merely *skilled*, Doc." Adam's voice rumbled with wonder. Eve couldn't speak. David's mouth actually dropped open.

A deep bark and the scraping clatter of claws echoed from the depths of the other end. In seconds, a black-and-tan German Shepherd raced to them, his eyes alert for danger but his mouth open in a canine smile and his tail wagging. Adam tensed beside her, as if ready to defend her against another attack.

"Puppy!" Eve exclaimed and dropped to her knees to wrap her arms around the fur tornado yipping and yelping in happiness. "Who's a good boy? Who's a handsome boy?"

Several moments passed before the dog calmed enough to sit, quivering with excitement and lapping at her face while she scratched his ears and thumped his sides. She glanced at Dr. Farrow, trying not to giggle as the dog switched to sniffing her ear. "He's gorgeous. Where did you get him?"

Dr. Farrow shook his head as if amazed. "That, dear Eve, is Apollo. He's a retired police dog. Injured in the line of duty and fitted with cybernetic limbs, like these two first-responders." He jerked his thumb toward David and Adam. "Unlike them, the rehabilitation didn't go well and he was scheduled to be euthanized. I got wind of it and adopted him. I've spent countless hours on his rehabilitation, but admit I don't have the energy he needs from an owner. And it appears he's taken a liking to you."

Eve turned back to the tongue-lolling face inspecting her. "Hello, Apollo. A pleasure to meet you. I'm Eve." He swiped her with his tongue again then circled her quickly, coming to heel at her left side, staring at her expectantly.

Adam reached a hand to help her stand. "You did say we should get a big dog for home defense. I think this one's chosen you."

She tangled her fingers in Apollo's coat and rubbed her lips together as she considered Adam's words. And his expression. It mirrored many of the looks he'd given her since the attack at the park. Intense but soft, shy yet confident. Happy. All the trouble she'd brought to his doorstep, and he was happy? The change sent champagne bubble tingles through her blood, although it also confused the hell out of her. She canted her head. "What is it?"

He smiled, and the full force of it nearly knocked her over. She couldn't remember ever having seen him truly smile before. He brushed a quick kiss across her cheek and squeezed her hand. "I'll tell you later."

Dr. Farrow waved them further into the bunker before sealing the door behind them. "My friends, why don't we whip up a quick dinner and I'll outline my plan while we break bread together."

They strolled to the massive kitchen, Apollo on her leg like static cling. Like he needed that constant connection. Or like he'd been trained to do. He hovered at the corner of the kitchen while they prepared a simple charcuterie platter—David decried the lack of crudité, winking at her—Apollo's gaze never leaving her. When she took her plate and sat at the dining table large enough for a party, he lay at her feet. She couldn't resist stroking his head and tickling his ears when he lifted his face to her. She'd never had a pet before. When Apollo rested his chin on her thigh and gazed at her with adoring eyes, she couldn't remember any of the lame excuses she'd used over the years for not getting one.

"Looks like another dopey male has fallen in love with you." Adam murmured in her ear as he took the seat next to her.

Shock hit her like a bullet. Had Adam just professed—? No, that couldn't be. She'd been nothing but trouble for him, upending his life and nearly getting him killed. He was probably joking. Although he had referred to her as his girlfriend earlier. That signified something, didn't it? That they were in a relationship at least. And not just because they'd had sex. Grown adults could have sex without the requirement that there be any sort of relationship status attached to it. Right? If Adam's choice of car, furniture, and reading material was any indication, he preferred the older things. Maybe that preference included relationship labels.

She reined in her galloping heart. Just because she loved Adam didn't mean she should go looking for proof that he loved her in return. Yes, he'd gone out of his way to protect her, but that was the kind of man he was. That was the officer in him. He no doubt missed the job, and keeping her safe was one way to reclaim that part of his life. She'd be a fool to read more into his actions and words than this.

He rested his hand on the back of her neck, his fingers gently caressing and squeezing, stoking the embers of last night's lovemaking. The stress tension in her muscles morphing into a tension far more pleasant. And demanding. She turned her head toward his, and his gaze dropped to her lips. Memories of last night bombarded her and she clenched her thighs to stem the need flowing there. Maybe she could take Adam up on his silent offer and sneak one more little kiss before—

"I'm sorry to interrupt." Farrow coughed as he sat across from them. He didn't look sorry. Neither did David, who sat next to the doc, his dark eyes sparkling with humor. Farrow continued. "I'll get right to it. There's a war going on, and cybernetic individuals are at the center of it."

The three of them sobered at the statement, glancing at each other, the good humor in the room evaporating. Eve's gut dropped to her feet. How could the doctor know what she knew? She swallowed. "I know. Preditech refuses to do anything about the problem with their cybernetic systems, and cyborgs are dying as a result."

Farrow was already shaking his head. "No, my dear. This is bigger than Preditech. In fact, I'd hazard a guess that the information you have on that mini-drive is fake."

"Fake? But I saw the file myself, in our CEO's network directory. It proves Preditech has consciously chosen not to fix the fatal flaw in their product. I downloaded it to the drive myself."

Farrow set his fork on his plate and folded his hands on the table. "I'm not denying what you think you have. That file may contain legitimate information. But at best, it's merely a smoke-screen... a diversion from what's actually going on. As a former surgeon who was initially brought in to help alpha-phase volunteers adapt to their new cybernetic enhancements, over the years I've noticed... things."

"What sort of things, Doc?" Adam urged, his hand still cupping Eve's neck. The warmth and comfort of his touch a balm for the thoughts ricocheting in her head.

"Subtle codes in CPU updates that seem questionable. Slight policy changes for rehabilitation which open up the possibility for a… perversion… of the program's original intent. Imperceptible re-structuring of oversight at the government level. And the growing feeling that something shady is going on." He opened his hands in a show he had nothing to hide. "If you want, I'm happy to walk you through the evidence I have, not one piece of which proves anything. But all of it put together, as a whole, paints a dark picture for our cybernetic friends."

"No offense, Doc. But you sound like a paranoid conspiracy theorist." David placed a hand on Doc's forearm.

Farrow barked out a laugh, patting David's hand and squeezing it. "I certainly feel like one sometimes. I fit another piece of the puzzle in and worry that I've lost my marbles completely. Look around at my tricked-out fallout shelter and my mad scientist lab, and it's obvious I'm not an average civilian. But, what's happening isn't your average corporate or government corruption."

Eve turned to Adam. "You were smart to believe this was bigger than just Preditech."

"Smart? Or lucky?" He shrugged, his gaze meaningful, reminding her of a conversation where he'd called her out on her assumption that luck and intelligence were diametrically opposed. He turned back to Farrow. "So, someone or some organization is working a major coup behind the scenes, and it involves cyborgs. To what end?"

"And why cyborgs?" David added. "We obviously glitch too much to be reliable for much of anything."

Farrow looked at David. "Have you ever glitched before today?"

David paused to think, then shook his head, still clearly befuddled about how and why he'd ended up in Adam's house. Farrow nodded as if he'd received the answer he expected. "Why do you assume what happened today was a glitch, especially if you've never experienced one before? I suggest you were given a command to break into Adam's house and attack Eve."

"But our cybernetic systems have failsafe commands—"

"Which can be overridden with the integration of new system updates. You know, those random downloads you're supposed to get. And I would imagine they can force an upload as easily as they download."

"Meaning they know what we know?" When Farrow nodded, David dropped his face into his hand, muttering curses.

Ice pulsed through Eve's veins. If what Farrow said was even half true, the problem was much bigger than she'd thought. How much power could be wielded by having access to thousands of cyborgs? The possibility was terrifying. And if there was a chance her actions could expose them or screw things up… Her gut clenched. "My god, access to all the cyborgs across the country… it's like a giant sleeper cell. No wonder they're trying to kill me."

Adam pulled her closer, as if sensing her need for his strength and comfort.

"Jesus, they can make us do anything." David groaned as if it was too much to handle, raking his hands through his hair. "Why are we here? They'll find out about you and make us kill you."

Farrow rubbed David's back, his voice softening to comfort the agitated man. "From what I figure, the modem link is the key. This facility has walls of thick concrete to prevent such a signal from coming or going. I removed your modem when you were out cold on the exam table, and did a diagnostic check to wipe out the kill command there, too. They can't get to you anymore."

David relaxed visibly at that news.

Adam spoke up. "I've been with Eve for days, Doc. Wouldn't I be the obvious choice to download a kill command to?"

"You are correct. And I can't explain why you weren't. Possibly you've experienced trauma to the modem or it's faulty."

"Like the rest of me." Adam snorted his disgust. "I glitch all the damn time."

Farrow scrubbed the back of his neck with his other hand. He bit his bottom lip, guilt apparent on his face. "Yes, well, remember when you came to see me that last visit, to inform me you were cured and didn't need me anymore? I jostled one of your power couplings so your systems would start to malfunction, hoping you'd contact me. But you're such a stubborn SOB, that it took nearly a decade, and this lovely woman, to get you to come around."

Eve laughed. Laughed at the dumbfounded look on Adam's face. Laughed at the absurdity of their situation. Laughed because otherwise she might cry if she thought too hard about what all this meant for her, for the men in this room, for cyborgs.

Apollo rested his head on her lap, maybe sensing the upheaval of her emotions. Adam kissed her temple and inhaled deeply against her hair. She leaned into him, loving the comfort he offered. Loving him.

Farrow rested his forearms on the table. "Adam, I can fix what I did. And I can remove your modem, so there's no worry about it going online. Truthfully, your inability to receive kill commands is probably why our Eve is still alive, and why David was sent to finish the job."

"You mean..." Adam straightened in surprise, pulling away from Eve. She placed her hand on his thigh to offer her silent support. "I thought my body and parts were past their prime and I was one glitch away from death, and all this time, it was an easy fix?"

"Yes. I'm sorry if you feared you were dying. But I did tell you to contact me if you needed me." Farrow had the grace to look contrite. He leaned forward. "I don't believe your glitches were ever life-threatening"—he glanced at Eve and frowned—"to yourself, anyway. I believe that, over time, the organic body and the cybernetic systems merge together. That one feeds the other, and just as an injured brain often rewires itself, the brain and processor reprogram each other. The same with the body. Your cybernetic systems should actually strengthen the rest of you."

"You mean, like how I never catch a cold? And how my right arm is almost as strong as my left?"

"Exactly. Of course, I haven't been able to prove this theory. I would need to dissect a cybernetic specimen, and there aren't many volunteers for that."

"Let's keep it that way, please." Eve paused as the simulated sunlight on the dome sky faded to night and lamps around the space automatically turned on, giving their little dinner party a festive summer barbecue ambiance. The atmosphere was such a stark contrast to their dire conversation, she hesitated to continue. "So, Dr. Farrow, you take a huge risk in telling us all this. Why trust us with these secrets? With the location of your Bat Cave? And what's your proposition you mentioned?"

"My dear, I spent years with these two. Stood next to them when they were at their worst. I know the kind of fighters they are, the kind of men they are. I trust them with my life. And I doubt Adam would have stood by you through this if you were any less worthy yourself." He paused, looking at the three of them. "As for my proposition, I would like the three of you to join me. Live in this shelter and work with me to help protect cybernetic individuals from a heretofore unknown enemy."

"What? Like The Justice League or The Avengers?" Adam asked.

Farrow shrugged. "I was thinking more like a Rebel Alliance fighting the imperial tyrants trying to control cyborgs. Together we could bring them down."

"We hope." David interjected, crossing his arms and shaking his head.

Farrow leaned closer to David, as if his proximity to bolster the man's confidence. "Rebellions are built on hope, my dear boy."

They stared at the doctor for a few minutes, each no doubt lost in their own thoughts and weighing the possibilities. Eve knew her answer. She was reportedly already dead, and had become that way by making it her mission to save cyborgs. Her mission simply became more official by helping Farrow. But Adam had a job and a home. And, once relieved of the drama she'd brought to his doorstep, he could go back to it.

Her heart clenched. What could be worse than dying? Helping Farrow, knowing that Adam had chosen to return to his old life without her.

David answered Farrow first. "I already admitted I don't have a life, Doc. By helping you, I'll at least have a purpose again. Count me in."

Farrow's face lit up. He turned hopeful eyes to Eve and Adam.

"Me, too." She choked out, staring at her hands, unable to look to her side, yet feeling Adam's gaze on her like a physical touch. She didn't have the courage to return the look. The fear of seeing his face, knowing by his expression that he would decline to join, was more debilitating than any of the life-threatening situations she'd yet encountered.

After what felt like an eternity, Adam exhaled loudly. "Without Eve, I'd still be a cyborg slowly dying on the inside, in more ways than one. Where she goes, I go."

The finality of his voice wrenched her heart. "No!" She forced her gaze to his, tears making the image watery. "Don't. You're not obligated to do this. You can go back to your life—"

"What life?" His laugh was bitter. "Stand around and twiddle my thumbs until I finally glitch enough to die?"

"Dr. Farrow said he can fix you. Then you go back to your home. Redecorate. Pick up another lost soul on a busy Saturday night and find someone to share your life with."

"Oh, darlin'." Adam shook his head and cupped her face with his warm hands, wiping at her tears with his thumbs. "Why should I do any that, when I have everything I want right here?"

He kissed her before she could respond. A slow, meaningful kiss, like a punctuation mark. A period at the end of their discussion. The final say in the argument. He smiled against her lips. "Besides, you owe me some boo-boo kisses."

Adam wrapped his arm around Eve and pulled her to his chest. Her heart tripped, and her brain couldn't—or was afraid to—wrap itself around the true meaning of Adam's declaration. He spoke to Farrow. "You said we could stay here?"

"Absolutely. There are plenty of rooms, each with private bathrooms, over against that wall. And, fortunately for us, they're also soundproof."

David snorted. Adam cleared his throat. Eve held him tighter.

Farrow stood and gathered their empty plates. David followed him into the kitchen where they worked together to load the dishwasher. David's voice carried to the dining area. "So, Doc. Care to, uh, show me the fire safety systems? I'd like to inspect the sprinkler hoses."

"Oh, that's a marvelous idea." Farrow's voice was slightly breathless. "And, perhaps, given our new circumstances, you should call me Timothy."

"Mmm-hmm. In that case, Timothy, I believe we should also redefine our doctor-patient relationship."

Doc exhaled a happy sigh. "That… that would be delightful, David."

Eve smiled as their voices faded into the distance. She turned her head toward Adam. "I think we're a bad influence on those two."

Adam kissed her again, the knuckles on his cyborg hand brushing against her nipples so she caught her breath. "There's nothing bad about finding the right person to love."

She jerked back, heart racing and unsure she'd heard him

correctly. Dare she hope he wasn't just talking about David and Farrow? Could she stand the answer if he was? Could she bear to keep living in this state of not knowing what feelings, if any, he had for her? Whether or not they had a future together? She swallowed hard, this conversation more nerve-wracking than the thought of another attack on her life. Because not knowing was slowly killing her. "What did you say?"

"I said…" He smiled again, the full wattage of that sexy curve stealing her breath. His fingers brushed the hair from her face. "I love you."

Angels sang and butterflies danced and the Earth tilted on its axis. Adam Lehmann loved her. And that truth was a powerful elixir, warming her body, mind, and soul so that she wanted to laugh and cry and sing and dance and shout to the world that the most amazing man loved her.

Instead, she held her head high and replied with all the dignity the moment deserved. Okay, she slanted him a knowing look and winked, trying not to laugh. "I know."

Chapter Twenty-Five

Adam stared at the examination table where Farrow was going to supposedly fix him. Assuming that would be as easy as the doc made it sound. Maybe it wouldn't. His back tingled and his Spidey-senses blared. His nerves were on edge, understandably so, because the last time he'd been on an operating table, he'd been dying and had signed his life away.

That choice had ultimately brought him here, to the moment where a beautiful woman he loved more than his own life had her arms wrapped around his torso and her luscious body pressed to his side, smiling at him like the sun rose and set with him. After the hell and sheer tedium he'd suffered, he couldn't regret a thing as she pressed her lips to his again.

But that didn't mean he relished going under the knife again.

"How's this going to work, Doc?"

Farrow was setting up the operation area, lining out his instruments and stacking gauze pads on a tray. "I'll open the service panel right above the first thoracic nerve. That will allow me to reach both the coupling and the modem with the smallest incision. I'll numb the area, but need you awake so you can report any system changes, just in case."

Farrow glanced at Eve and David. "You two might want to step outside."

David raised his hands in surrender. "Give me a three-alarm fire any day, but blood makes me woozy. I'll go to up top and inspect the water system in the warehouse."

Farrow nodded, his gaze lingering on David's departing back for a few heartbeats before turning to Eve. "There will be blood, my dear."

Eve shook her head and held tighter to Adam. "Doc, he finally admitted he loves me. I'm not letting him out of my sight for a long while."

"I figured as much." Farrow's smile was downright smug. The man had a gift of being able to read people. "Grab a chair. I'll need you seated on the other side holding his hand."

Adam pulled his shirt off and tossed it onto an empty counter. He climbed onto the operating table, hissing when the cold padding contacted his skin. The adjustable table could have easily doubled as a massage chair with its cushioned surface and a hole near the top for his face. He stared at the sterile tile floor, his heart pounding a break-neck speed, his nerves taut. Only sheer willpower, and the soft comfort of Eve's hand holding his, stilled the urge to leap off and run the other way.

Gritting his teeth, he commanded his nerves to chill the fuck out. This surgery wasn't anything like the one he'd had before. He wasn't even going to be sedated. Farrow was the best and Adam trusted him with his life. Most importantly, he wouldn't have to worry ever again about glitching and accidentally hurting Eve.

He had no reason to be this uneasy.

Eve's warm lips brushed against his bare shoulder. He lifted his head enough to turn and kiss her. What he wouldn't give to pull her body under his and make love to her as thoroughly as he had last night before they both fairly passed out from exhaustion. But he recognized the delay tactic for what it was, and squelched the urge to deepen the kiss. Plus, Farrow had already placed a blood pressure monitor on a finger, and pricked the back of his neck with local anesthesia.

Farrow wasn't giving him a chance to wimp out.

Eve gave him a quick squeeze. "You're in good hands." She smiled and took her spot next to him, tugging her surgical mask in place. Adam sighed, squeezed her hand in return, and settled his face back into the padding, drawing in deep, calming breaths.

"Adam, you're doing great." Farrow's voice was muffled behind his surgical mask. "Now, I'm poking you with the dull end of my scalpel. Can you feel it?"

"No."

"Okay, now I'm pinching with a pair of tweezers. Can you feel that?"

"No."

"Very good. Now I'm going to cut away a flap of skin. If at any point you feel pain, try not to flinch. Give Eve's hand a hard squeeze and I'll give you more anesthesia."

Adam's nerve endings registered nothing but the pressure of Farrow's scalpel against his back, and a trickle of warmth along his shoulder which was followed by a broad swipe. No doubt that was Farrow wiping blood from the incision.

Silence except for the sound of three people breathing and the moist sucking of Farrow fiddling around the muscles and wires in his back. Adam focused on inhaling and exhaling in a steady manner, and the two points of warmth where Eve held his hand and rested her other on his shoulder.

A soft click and he felt rather than heard the collective sigh of relief from Eve and Farrow. "Okay Adam, I've removed the chip." The tension in his muscles swept away like a leaf in the rain.

Farrow continued. "You got a lot of carbon scoring here. And a bit of calcification around the connectors. I'll have to scrape it away before I readjust your power couplings."

Adam's modem was out. Eve was safe. Even if Farrow didn't fully cure his glitches, at least Adam couldn't download a command to kill her. Anything else was icing on the cake.

"Okay, Doc."

"Very good. This will only take me a minute."

As Farrow fiddled some more, Eve rubbed her thumb across the back of Adam's hand in an almost tantric rhythm. He matched his breathing to the slow path back and forth. Back and forth. Inhale. Exhale. His vision narrowed to a gray speck in the floor's neutral pattern, and his world narrowed to Eve's touch. Farrow murmured a pleased note, and Adam heard the quiet snap of the connector locking into place.

His world went red.

Adam rolled to the side, knocking Farrow away. Readings scrolled down the peripheral of his tunnel vision, like stats from a video game. Health. Heart rate. Maps. Weaponry. Weaponry? He tried to apologize to Farrow, but couldn't move his mouth or make words.

He swung his legs off the side, seeking Eve's comfort. No, not her comfort. Her life. He jumped off the table and wrapped his left hand around her throat. Slowly squeezing it. Her eyes bulged, and she clawed at his fingers.

His heart clenched and his brain screamed. He was choking Eve. Killing her. Her struggles pointless. He tried to stop. He tried to open his hand. *WHY THE HELL WAS HE KILLING HER?*

FUCK! A command code must have gotten through and his body moved as if it belonged to someone else. Those bastards would pay. But Eve would pay the ultimate price. By his own hand.

He concentrated on his cyborg hand. Imagined releasing her throat. He was not a machine. He wasn't a toaster that did whatever it was programmed to do. He was a man. A man with fancy prosthetics. *HE* was the one in charge of his body, and *HE* demanded his body obey him. Commanded his body to *BACK THE FUCK DOWN!*

Eve stopped struggling. Her hands fell from his and her eyes looked at him, filled with love and tears. Love. She loved him.

And he loved her. How could he possibly kill her when he would give his life for her? He'd rather die than hurt her.

His grip slackened. She sucked in air.

His hand released her. She fell to her knees, coughing and dragging in ragged breaths.

He stepped away from her. The scrolling stats faded. His vision broadened, The red evaporated. He felt… like his normal self again. Felt—

He doubled over and his knees buckled as pain burst in his groin region. "What the fuck?" He ground out through clenched teeth.

Eve's laugh was high and brittle where she had collapsed on the floor, sucking in gulps of air. "I might have… kicked you in… the nuts to… stop you. You were… unreachable."

"That was… amazing." Farrow's stunned voice caught Adam's attention, and he turned toward where the doc stood with defibrillator paddles in each hand, frozen in shock by what he'd witnessed.

What had he witnessed? "No, not amazing! Fucking awful!" Adam yearned to help Eve, but was afraid to get near her again in case whatever it was happened again. Fists clenching his thighs where he kneeled on the floor, his fear and regret morphed into anger and he directed it at Farrow. "This was more than a glitch, Doc. You said you'd fixed me. Is this what you meant? Fixed me so I'd kill Eve? You said these concrete walls would keep out downloads. How the hell did this download happen? Is this what your so-called rebellion is about?"

"Adam, stop. Dr. Farrow isn't to blame." Eve pulled herself up.

Adam whirled on her, unable to weed through the emotions

rioting in his heart. "He isn't? Then who is? This is exactly what I warned you about." He rose, his fear for her safety outweighing the pain in his crotch, and took a step back. Needed to put distance between them so he couldn't grab her as easily next time. "I'll glitch and hurt you. I damn near killed you!"

"Yeah, I was there." She glared at him, but it seemed more of a glare because he was being obtuse than because he'd tried to murder her.

"Adam." Farrow's placating voice reached through the haze of Adam's distress. "I'm not sure what happened. Maybe there was a downloaded command stuck because of the calcification or the unconnected coupling. Whatever we did set a dormant command in motion."

Adam whirled on the doc again. "How can you be sure? How can you guarantee that I don't have any more kill codes floating around this thing"—he waved a hand to indicate his head—"that might someday find their way to the right spot and make me go rogue again?" All this time, he'd only worried about hurting someone because his arm might flex at the wrong time. The reality was more terrifying. One wrong command, and he would be a cyborg gunned down by an army of officers on a public street. One random code, and Eve would be a lifeless heap at his feet.

It was enough to make him vomit.

Farrow stepped over to Eve and placed a supporting arm around her shoulders. Adam cringed again. He should be the one offering her comfort. Instead, he was the cause for it.

"Do you trust me, Adam?" Farrow's tone was calm yet resolute. The same tone he'd often taken with Adam during rehabilitation. The memory of their frequent conversation almost a meditative *Ohm,* soothing him and bringing him back to his center.

Do you trust me, Adam?

Yeah, Doc. I trust you. I just don't trust myself.

Then you'll have to trust me when I say you will find your way through this.

"Adam." Farrow repeated. "Do you trust me?"

Adam sighed, long and low, despair poking at the new growth of his love for Eve. He heaved his shoulder in a shrug, staring at the doctor's shoes. "Yeah, Doc. I trust you. I just don't trust myself."

"I trust you." Eve's voice was a little hoarse from the recent choking, but firm and unwavering. Adam glanced at her. The delicate skin of her neck was already a garish purple where he'd tried to crush it. Yet her eyes were filled with love.

"You'll find your way through this. And we'll help." Farrow held a hand out to Adam. "I'll do a complete diagnostic on you. We'll root out any latent commands and make sure my fix to your power coupling worked. It may take several hours. But you'll be completely sure once we're finished."

Adam stared at Farrow, processing the offer. He wanted more than anything to be certain he would never be a threat to Eve again. He wanted to stop living in fear of his cybernetic systems. Wanted to get on with living his life instead of waiting for death.

He nodded. "Strap me down. And send Eve where she'll be safe."

Eve opened her mouth, probably to refuse to leave because that's how she was and why he loved her so much. Farrow shook his head, and Adam was grateful the doc was on his side in this. "My dear, it's going to be a long and tedious procedure, and very boring. You should return to the shelter. The entertainment choices are meager, but they'll be more interesting than this."

Eve looked ready to argue, but finally relented. "Fine. I'll go. But if you're not down by dinnertime, I'm coming back for both of you."

She turned to Adam and speared him with a fierce look even as her voice quivered. "When this is all over and the doctor has given you a clean bill of health, you will *never* again whine about possibly hurting me, you hear? And you *will* make it through to come back to me because"—She inhaled a tremulous breath, tears shining in her eyes like stars—"because you owe me some serious boo-boo kisses."

She jabbed a finger at her throat as if he didn't know exactly what boo-boo she meant. Then she whirled and stomped out of the room, muttering something about love and stupid cyborgs.

Once she walked that lush ass of hers through the door and out of his eyesight, Adam pulled his gaze to Farrow. The doctor contemplated him in return. "You know, your love for that woman is what saved her. You were able to override the command in your CPU. You did what no cybernetic individual thinks they can do."

"Yeah, so?"

"So, if you can consciously override a command, they no longer control you. The threat of rogue cyborgs becomes a myth… a fairy tale with little impact except for its entertainment value. Like *Sleeping Beauty* or *Beauty and the Beast.*"

Adam shook his head and climbed back on the exam table like climbing the steps to the gallows. "Fine. Just promise me we won't break out into song and dance."

Chapter Twenty-Six

"They still at it?" David strolled into the cozy backyard oasis formed by rattan lounge chairs with turquoise cushions and dotted by tangerine throw pillows. Trellised cherry tomato plants created an intimate perimeter. Through the entrance, Eve could view the shelter door. Not that she'd been staring at it, willing it to open and Adam to walk through, or anything.

Eve glanced up from where she sat, an exhausted Apollo at her side. She'd tried to keep her mind busy so she didn't think about what Adam and Dr. Farrow were doing. Which meant the poor dog had spent the day training and chasing balls. He'd loved it, and was worn out. He slept hard, his ears barely flicking at David's approach.

David had taken a shower and changed clothes, his hair still damp and his feet bare. He stood with his hands in his pockets, waiting for her to answer. But she had no answer. Not any real answers. Only hope. And fear.

"What was it like, David? When you were under the control of the kill command?"

With a long sigh, he sat on the edge of a nearby seat,

chuffing his arms as if to warm them even though the shelter was a pleasant seventy-two degrees. "It, uh, was like I was watching someone else. Like a first-person video game. One moment, I'm in control of myself, and the next moment, I'm watching myself lunge for you to kill you, my head screaming to my body to stop. I wasn't in control, even though I felt all the punches Adam landed. The crazy part is that I only have a cyborg leg and some synthetic vertebrae in my lower back, all connected to the core processor." He waved a hand toward the back of his neck where she'd disabled him with water and Farrow had pulled his modem. "That shouldn't be enough to go rogue with, but I did. I'm thinking there's something to Timothy's theory about the organic/synthetic integration."

He shrugged and stood. He paused a moment before clearing his throat. "Listen, Eve. I want to thank you, and Adam, for not killing me. It would have been the easier thing to do."

Eve had an answer for this, even though David hadn't asked a question. "No, it wouldn't have been the easier choice." She gazed past David to scowl at the shelter door. "I set out to help save all cyborgs, not just the stubborn ones who can't take their head out of their ass long enough to realize nobody's perfect, everyone makes mistakes and they'll be forgiven, but they need to learn to forgive themselves as well."

"He's a lucky man to have you on his side." David chuckled. He jerked his head to indicate the kitchen. "I'm going to start dinner. Harvested some fresh veggies upstairs and I'm going to make *pico de gallo* and burritos. Join me if you want to chat."

She buried her fingers in Apollo's silky coat. "I'm not really hungry. And I'm sure I'm not very good company right now."

"Eve, a watched pot never boils. And a watched door never opens."

She sighed. He was right. And she'd spent enough time moping. Careful not to wake Apollo, she stood. "I'll chop while you give me the details about this homeless outreach program Doc has."

"Deal. Timothy is a total genius." David's eyes lit up as he led the way to the kitchen.

She's obviously touched on his favorite topic and was pretty sure it wasn't the outreach program. David carried the conversation while they worked together to make dinner. Apollo trotted in at one point, and sat next to her as she chopped, sliced, and diced everything David handed her. As the ingredients came together and the end of meal-preparation loomed, Eve's nerves twitched. She'd promised to retrieve Adam and Farrow if they weren't back by dinner. But there hadn't been a peep from either. What if something had gone wrong? What if another latent kill command had been triggered and Farrow was dead? He had coded them into the entry system. Adam could walk through that door and finish what his commands had started.

Eve touched her neck where he'd choked her. She'd seen it in the bathroom mirror earlier. Dark bruises. It hurt to swallow, and her voice was still gravelly. When Adam had first wrapped his hand around her neck and squeezed, she'd struggled, clawing and gasping for air. Then she'd realized the internal battle he must have been waging. His cyborg hand was strong enough to snap her neck, but he hadn't. And his grip had been loose enough she could suck in little bits of oxygen. So she'd worked to be calm and conserve her air, waiting for the Adam she loved to overpower the cyborg he feared.

And he had.

But it wasn't enough for him. He needed proof. Proof she hoped the doctor had given him. Proof she feared didn't exist because he was belligerent enough to still question it.

She rinsed her knife off as the shelter door hissed and swung open. Her heart jumped to her throat and she whipped around to see what outcome would greet her. Adam stepped through, his face tight with rage. Dear god he, he was under a kill command again!

Terror zapped her strength, but she managed to reach for the sink's water hose and pull it in front of her, aimed and ready to spray when he was close enough.

Farrow stepped through, alive but exhausted.

Her knees gave out and she sank to the floor as Adam approached. Apollo guarded her front, ears alert. When Adam was close enough, Apollo's body tensed for the attack. No, wait, he simply sat and wagged his tail. Adam ran a hand over the dog's head, receiving a few happy licks in return.

"Dinner's ready, but it'll wait, Timothy." David said to Farrow, wrapping and arm around his shoulders and turning him toward the sleeping rooms. "First, you rest while I massage your back."

"That's sounds perfect, my dear David." Farrow sounded weary yet relieved.

Eve wasn't paying attention to them, her focus on Adam. He smiled at Apollo, but when his attention turned to her, his smile faded and his brows furrowed again. Why was he angry at her? She looked more closely. He wasn't angry, he was… tired. Uncertain?

Had the diagnostic been successful or not? What was wrong? Why wasn't he happy?

Oh. Maybe because she'd pointed a water hose at him. And she hadn't yet smiled either. Maybe he simply mirrored her own concerned expression. Apollo lay next to her and rested his chin on her thigh. She brushed a hand over his head, her gaze never leaving Adam as he kneeled in front of her. He didn't speak or break eye contact, until his gaze dipped to her neck, his expression darkening at the sight. At the reminder of what could have happened. But hadn't. She drew in a breath to remind him of that, when he held something out to her. She tore her gaze from his to look at it. Something small wrapped in color paper and sitting atop a candy stick. A lollipop. A specific brand, to be exact.

She lifted her gaze back to his. "Are you trying to tell me you're a Dum-Dum?"

He huffed a humorless laugh, nodding his head. "Well, Doc didn't have any Utter-Dumbass suckers to give out, so this will have to suffice. He also gave me a clean bill of health. No hidden commands, no weird codes. Just me. He also thinks my love for you was able to overpower the latent kill code that hit me."

"That's great. Why are you frowning?"

He sat in front of her, their knees touching, and drew in a deep breath. "Because I can't overpower the worry that you'll never forgive me and will leave. And that would destroy me more than anything. More than a shot of water from that kitchen sprayer. More than a bullet to the head."

She growled in frustration, wanting to kick some sense into him. "After everything we've been through? After me telling you I love you? Showing you how much I love you? Yes, I stuck with you because I didn't have anywhere else to go. But also because I trusted you. I knew that, with you next to me, we'd be okay. Why can't you understand that?"

He spun the lollipop between two fingers and screwed his face up. "Because I'm a Dum-Dum?"

Eve crossed her arms over her chest and simply waited.

He dropped the lollipop and took her hand in his. In *both* of his. "Eve, I can't promise I won't screw up again and piss you off or make you want to choke me. I might be a cyborg, but I'm also human, and we tend to fuck up. Some of us more than others." He pointed a finger at his chest. "But I promise you, I will always work to be the best cybernetic human I can be, if you say you'll stay and be with me."

Her emotional dam broke, and she couldn't hold back her tears any longer. Her heart blossomed. The fear, the worry, and anger… everything but hope and love drained away, leaving her lighter than she'd felt in longer than she could remember. Her sexy cyborg loved her. They were on a path to help the other cyborgs. Neither she nor Adam were alone any more.

She reached for him, needing his strength and warmth. Needing the physical proof that this was happening, that he was real. Adam lifted her onto his lap and wrapped both arms around her, bathing her face in kisses, murmuring words of love and encouragement. She palmed his cheeks and kissed him deeply, pouring her love into one kiss so he'd never question her feelings toward him ever again.

Pulling back just enough to look into his eyes, Eve smiled. "I promise to stay and be with you, Adam Lehmann." She took his lips in a quick kiss. "I love you."

His smile lit the room brighter than the sun on the shelter's ceiling. He winked at her. "I know."

Chapter Twenty-Seven

Epilogue

"Here's a package for Doc, Miss Eve." The vagrant wearing tattered clothes the same color of dirt-brown as his uncombed hair and beard, handed a delivery box over the fold-up table toward her.

She laid it at her feet by where Apollo sat at attention, then motioned to the baskets of vegetables which threatened to topple the rickety setup. "Thank you, Charlie. Please help yourself to some vegetables. Or, if you prefer fruit, you're welcome to pick some. The blueberries and raspberries are ripe."

Charlie plucked a couple potatoes and shoved them into the deep pockets of his overcoat and chuckled. "When the doc starts growing cheeseburgers and whiskey, I'll consider working the harvest. Sure could use another length of that wire Doc gave me last time, though."

The homeless individuals who came to HydroFoods for fruits and vegetables from Doc's plentiful warehouse always traded with something. She'd only helped out for a few days, but Eve suspected these weren't mere vagrant individuals. They were possibly a network of spies Doc had built over the years. More of his Rebel Alliance. Feeding the homeless and donating his time and skill as a doctor to the indigent population, especially plentiful in this abandoned part of town, was a brilliant way to cover up his need for things like medical and mechanical equipment. Like the generator that had arrived yesterday. And the contraceptive implant he'd ordered for her this morning.

Living completely off the grid would be impossible for anyone who was trying to subvert whoever was after cyborgs, but this was the next best thing.

She smiled at the homeless man. Charlie likely wasn't even his real name. "I'll make a note of that and be sure to pass it along to Doc. You have a wonderful day. I hope you can come for spaghetti dinner next week. I can't promise whiskey, but there will be brownies."

He nodded at her, then toward the package at her feet. "There's a little something for you in there as well." He palmed a carrot and hunkered away toward the public entrance, nibbling on the orange root.

Eve glanced outside, through the open receiving dock doors, seeing no one in the vicinity but Charlie's retreating form. Most of their customers arrived in the relatively cooler morning hours on harvest days. The sunlight simulator, combined with the skylights dotting the ceiling, provided the plants with all they needed for photosynthesis. But the fresh air, even if it was a muggy August afternoon, was a welcome change for everyone.

Still, she wiped at the sweat on her neck with a towel and took a drink of water. Sitting, she tickled Apollo's ears and picked up the package, turning it in her hands. It looked like any overnight delivery package addressed to Farrow, and was still sealed. How could it have anything for her, and how could Charlie know about it?

"What's that? Another package for Doc?" Adam appeared at her side and grabbed the towel to wipe his face. He and David had spent the day building planters for trees, so HydroFoods could offer a wider variety of fruit, and he had certainly worked up a sweat. Eve stared at him, loving the way the light shined on his glistening muscles and highlighted his tattoos. He had removed his shirt, and his jeans slung low on his hips, teasing her with a delicious hint of what it covered.

She smiled at him. "Nope. That package is all mine."

"Watch yourself, Darlin'." His deep rumble sent shivers to her sensitive spots. "Or I might bend you over that rain barrel for a quick tryst."

He leaned down and kissed her exactly the way she liked it. Long, lingering, full of promise for more later. Then murmured against her lips. "Which is a shame. I'd much rather have you splayed naked in our bed, hot and screaming for hours."

Oh, thank goodness for soundproof rooms. They made facing Doc and David each morning bearable. Although Eve suspected those two were too busy making their own cries of pleasure to hear anyone else's. Still, Eve glanced at the rain barrel, mushing her lips and contemplating taking Adam up on both of his offers.

"Oh, is that a package from Charlie?"

Doc's voice decided for her. Rain barrel would have to wait. She turned to the approaching man walking hand-in-hand with a sweaty and shirtless David and held the package out. "Yes. He said there was also something in here for me, which doesn't make sense. He also requested some more wire."

Nodding, Doc took the package and opened it. "Yes, I expected Charlie would need more wire. I'll be sure to get him some. Now what have we here?"

He pulled out a brick-sized lump, wrapped in paper and tied with twine.

They leaned in to watch. David glanced at Doc. "Is it your birthday?"

Doc chuckled and shook his head as he unwrapped the lump. When the pages peeled away, he held... a brick. A plain household brick, worn, with cracks and chips and leaving a layer of dust and dirt in his hand.

Eve hadn't known Doc as long as the others, but even she knew he didn't do anything without a reason, as if he planned ten steps out, with twenty contingency plans. None of them wanted to play chess with the man, that was for certain. "Doc, why would you need a brick?"

He hefted it in his palm, then set it on the table. "I don't. But Charlie needed something to weight the package down. What really came for me is this." He waved the papers in his hands, then glanced through them, nodding and grunting in assent.

He handed them to Eve. "Remember when I said we should start looking for cybernetic individuals I helped rehabilitate? Especially the ones who have fallen off the grid like Adam and David? If we could find them and gain their trust, we can begin to build that wave of rebellion? I think we found our starting point."

He said no more, merely watched her like he expected her to do something. So she looked at the sheets of paper. Each sheet listed dozens of names, presumably of cyborgs who had worked with Doc over the years. Some names had information next to them, like address and other names, possibly family or friends, and what she surmised were employers, either present or past. And a few names had pictures next to them. Whoever Doc had outsourced this research to, they were good.

They were probably Charlie.

Eve continued to scan the names and whatever information had been unearthed, noting the ones with pictures. Why would Doc want her to peruse the information? If these were cyborgs who had rehabilitated here in Indianapolis, they were likely locals. She was from Chicago. She wouldn't know any of—

Her gaze caught on one of the listed cyborgs, and she reread the information. Name. Employer. And a picture. She glanced at Doc, who seemed to already know what she was going to say. "I know this person."

She glanced at the page once more, blinking because she

didn't believe it. Was she imagining things? But when she looked again, the information had not changed. A picture, a face. A familiar face. A woman, with bold red lips and cat-eyeliner, her red hair tied back with a flowered scarf. Next to it, *Hayworth, Betty. Greater Broad Ripple Public Library.*

About the Author

Ava Cuvay is an award-winning, bestselling author who writes out of this world Sci-fi Romance featuring sassy heroines, gutsy heroes, passion, adventure, and an alcoholic beverage or two... often set in a galaxy far, far away. She resides in central Indiana with her own scruffy-looking nerfherder, teens who don't realize just how cool she is, and two kitties that make her laugh. She believes life is too short to bother with negative people, everything is better with Champagne, and Han Solo shot first.

Sign up for an Exclusive Bonus Scene and More Book News!

Join my newsletter for an exclusive bonus scene, freebies, Advanced Reader Copy opportunities, and fun info! https://drink ingthestarspressllc.eo.page/cbq6y

Stalk Me!

Check me out and follow me on your preferred platform:
Website for a complete listing of her books: AvaCuvay.com
Facebook Page: AvaCuvayAuthor
Goodreads Page: https://www.goodreads.com/author/show/15051407.Ava_Cuvay
BookBub: https://www.bookbub.com/authors/ava-cuvay
Amazon Author Page: https://www.amazon.com/Ava-Cuvay/e/B01E5OIZ0I/

Please Leave a Review!

Book reviews are one of the few ways we authors receive feedback from our readers. And we hunger for it! Please take a few minutes and leave a review this book. Thank you!

"Tin Toy" Sneak Peek

Betty Hayworth leaned back against the tufted cushion of the library loveseat, a holo-book clutched to her chest as she reveled in the emotional satisfaction of the twenty-first century historical romance she'd just finished. She hadn't understood much of the period slang—the antagonist had been *sus,* the couple had been *shipped,* the adventure *YOLO'd,* and all manner of items *yeeted* —but that had not lessened her enjoyment.

As if to prove her own point, a contented sigh escaped her lips.

She loved books, a passion supported by her job as director of a small neighborhood library in the eclectic, upscale Greater Broad Ripple area of Indianapolis, Indiana. She especially loved romance novels. Genre didn't matter; she read them all. Small towns, big cities, Regency England, even futuristic space opera. As long as the hero realized he wanted the heroine more than power, wealth, prestige, vengeance, or the family farm. As long as he vowed to stand beside her no matter life threw at them.

That's what she loved about romance novels. Passionate kisses. Hot sex. A swoon-worthy love interest.

And a happily-ever-after.

Because in this day and age, finding happily-ever-after was a real challenge for many individuals, most especially cybernetic individuals like her. Depression. Suicide. Glitches. Angry mobs of terrified citizens. Society in the twenty-second century tolerated cyborgs and cybernetic sympathizers about as much as Salem in the 1600s had liked witches.

Therefore, a vital ingredient to achieve her own happily-ever-after was not being outed as a cyborg.

Which made family, friends, and romantic relationships oddly detrimental to a happily-ever-after goal. Even for a happy-for-now goal.

Fortunately, Betty didn't have any of those detriments. Also fortunately, she didn't need them. Except for the rare occasion when she longed for human interaction more meaningful than recommending books to her library patrons, she had ready access to millions of characters who filled that void in her life. And not risk her own life in the process.

"Thank the Maker I love to read." She murmured into the quiet coziness of her neighborhood library, then glanced at the holo-book still in her hands. The *rom-com* story and its bumbling hero still circled around her brain and gripped her heart. "Otherwise, I wouldn't have you to add to my ever-growing list of book boyfriends, Mr. Tall-Dark-and-Social-Media-Influencer… whatever that is."

Betty uncurled from the cozy loveseat and slipped into her leopard print pumps with the red bows. She left her empty teacup on the side table and returned the book to the stack of new arrivals she'd received yesterday. One caught her eye and punched her gut in unison. The latest from a popular author of political cyborg thrillers, a regular patron had requested it. Otherwise, Betty wouldn't have ordered it. Ever. Society hated cyborgs enough as it was, she didn't need to feed into the ugly stereotype of them as unhinged psychopaths or emotionless killing machines.

Yet, she held a book depicting cyborgs in that exact manner.

Unlike the *futuristic* romance books from the previous century, today's authors never painted cyborgs as the heroes or the love interests. They were the villains, and the villains always lost in the end.

She'd personally lived that particular truth for the past several years and didn't need the reminder stacked among the library's shelves. Didn't want to face those patrons who checked out the book—a book she admittedly judged by its horrid cover featuring a mangled cyborg—nor listen to those patrons talk about how wonderful the book was or how realistic the cybernetic antagonist.

"You might have to suffer an irreparable injury." She glared at the holo-book and shoved it to the side, battling a twinge of guilt for the threat. Taking her frustration out on library property would not change the world's opinion about cyborgs. Destroying the book wouldn't even hinder the author from writing another unpalatable cyborg-villain story. And her threat smacked of narrow-minded censorship, like the book burnings of centuries past. Freedom of opinion, the open exchange of ideas, was integral to her role as a librarian. She was the first line of defense against the tyranny of the thought police, the keeper of free speech. It was her superpower.

A superpower which conflicted with her secret existence as a public pariah.

She glanced around the homey little library which had once been someone's quaint two-story house complete with gingerbread trim and a white picket fence. Second-hand ottomans and tufted armchairs scattered amid floor-to-ceiling bookshelves. The murals painted on the front bay windows colored what little light they allowed inside, lending a dance-club vibe to the room. No, wrong imagery. The streams of rich rainbow hues, catching on the particles of floating dust, were more akin to the reverence of a church, especially in the muted quiet which accompanied it. Her own little oasis amid the noise of the city outside these walls. A tranquil refuge for the weary, wandering soul looking for respite. A gateway to thousands of worlds a person could explore from the safety and comfort of a cozy loveseat and cup of Earl Grey.

She rubbed her temples, the silence of the library a banging gong in her head. As much as she appreciated her quiet existence, maybe the monotony wore on her. A wistful thread of desire for friendly conversation with someone who wasn't a fictional character from a book wound through her heart. And a wave of desire for some interaction of a more physical nature wound through needier body parts, thanks in part to her recently enjoyed book. Family, friends, and romantic relationships might be detrimental to her safety as a cyborg, but she was still mostly human, and humans were social animals.

Other than the visit last week from the long-legged woman named Eve—the one who'd merely surfed the internet on the library computers and then raced out without a single good-bye, thank-you, or go to hell—Betty hadn't had a patron in weeks. And she hadn't been laid in years.

Loneliness reared its ugly mug on occasion, but such was a necessary side-effect of her plan: lay low and don't draw attention.

She snorted at the last bit. As if her pinup model couture from a bygone era could go unnoticed. Clothes emphasizing her curves and colors popping with knowing innocence, her appearance screamed *va-va-voom!* And her resting bitch face countered with *back off.* A nice balance, if anyone cared for her opinion, because it kept her safe, if a bit lonely and horny. But her appearance did not say *nothing to see here.*

On the up side, neither did it say *hey, I'm a cyborg.* Which was the crucial aspect of her *don't die* plan. She worked hard to keep her particular secret... well, a secret. If she was ever discovered, loneliness and forced celibacy would be the least of her worries.

The bell above the front door chimed its cheerful welcome to an incoming customer. Betty hastened around the desk to the front of the building, nearly giddy to have someone to talk to and a distraction for her churning internal thoughts.

A young man stood at the front. A stocky twenty-something wearing trendy jeans and a concert tee, he smelled like automotive lubricant and yesterday's bar tab. His belligerent expression seemed odd for someone who entered a library of his own free will, but she recognized him as a result.

"Welcome to the Greater Broad Ripple Public Library. I'm Betty." She greeted him, pasting a bright smile on her face even though her gut clenched. At least this was an ice bath to the simmering arousal the romance novel had kindled. "You came to the poetry reading last month, didn't you? Paul, right?"

He'd been an asshole then. His expression bespoke the fact he would likely be an asshole again.

He shoved his fists into his front pockets and glared at her with eyes bleary and bloodshot. Come to think of it, he'd been similarly inebriated at the poetry reading. "Yeah. My girlfriend dragged me. Said it would be *romantic*"—that word spoken as if it was a slimy bug—"but it was just a bunch of women reading about their fucking periods and how men suck."

True, there had been some of that, but she wasn't about to encourage his attitude. She shrugged. "It was an open mic evening. Participants read the poetry which spoke to them. I'm sorry you didn't enjoy the selections they chose."

"Didn't go thinking I'd enjoy it. I went thinking it would get me laid. Instead, my girlfriend bitched at me until I'd had enough and dumped her ass."

He'd accompanied a sweet, petite blonde who'd chosen a

touching poem about the patience and absolution of love. While Betty couldn't judge how a person might act in a private setting, the young woman had not seemed the bitching type.

Still, Paul looked at Betty as if expecting a reaction to his crass words. She shrugged. "Um, congratulations?" Honestly, where was this conversation headed and why were they having it?

"The opposite. I work for her dad, and he fired me. Said it was because I was a drunk, but I know it's 'cuz she cried to him about me being a shitty boyfriend." Paul glared at the side room where the poetry reading had been stationed. "Shitty boyfriend, ha. I treated her good. She just doesn't like me drinking. Doesn't understand that I'm relaxing. I like to play hard when I'm not working."

"Well, I'm very sorry for your troubles." No, she wasn't. She walked to the front door and grasped the handle, turning back to address him. "But, this is a library. Not an AA meeting, dating resource, or staffing agency. I'm afraid we have nothing here to offer you."

Not true. The library had plenty of resources available for him to propel himself into a new career, relationship, or sobriety. She didn't even need to reference her CPU's body language database for proof he wanted a scapegoat, not a solution, so she opened the door and tilted her head toward it, clearly indicating he should leave.

He didn't.

Instead, he sauntered toward her, his gaze roving her from head to toe and all her assets in between as if he approved. As if she could rest easy now, assured she had acquired his endorsement. He licked his lips like she was a tasty morsel. She swallowed the groan and managed to refrain from rolling her eyes. Did he think that was sexy? Did he expect her to giggle, flip her hair, and yowl like a cat in heat?

The art of seduction was wasted on the young and inebriated.

He stopped in front of her, his whiskey breath wilting her pin curls and his eyes squarely focused on her chest. She wore a cropped cardigan over a boat-neck top, so there was no visible cleavage. However, short of wearing a cardboard box, she couldn't hide the ample curve of her breasts and he assumed that was an invitation to leer. "Nothing to offer me, huh? This is a library, and I'd like to check you out."

Her derisive snort came before she could stop it. She might be horny, but she wasn't desperate. Grateful the thought didn't rush out of her mouth like the snort had, she plunked a hand on a hip, and leaned on the door, her words clipped. "May-December romance tropes are out of favor at the moment. But if you're looking for reading materials, I'd recommend craft books on how to be more than a one-dimensional character. Or psychology books on what women want from a man, and—trust me—it's not to be ogled. These can all be checked out for two weeks with a valid local ID. But as for me, I just work here."

She flashed him her biggest *get-lost* smile and waved toward the outside.

Instead of taking the not-so-subtle hint, he blinked a few times while her words soaked into his 80-proof gray matter. He scowled. All the anger over his own inept life directed at her as if she was the cause for his woes. His hands fisted at his side. He tensed, ready to lunge at her, and growled. "Look here, you b—"

Betty stepped away, pretended to wobble and lose her balance, then slammed the edge of the door into his face. "Oh, heavens! I am so clumsy!" She feigned surprise and concern. Blood spurted from his nose and dribbled on his shirt before he could cover it with a hand or curse at her. She reached for him— "Goodness, let me help you with that."—and shoved him outside, then closed and locked the door.

"You want me to call an ambulance?" She yelled through the

wood door. Without waiting for a response, she walked back to the kitchen to brew another cup of tea. Hibiscus this time, to celebrate. She might be a librarian, but her real superpower was ousting assholes.

"Tin Toy" Available at your favorite online retailer: https://books2read.com/b/49LO7Y